In memory of Louise B. Moore,
who made journalism a proud profession

D0179479

Acknowledgments

I relied on many friends and relations to research this book. They included Deanna Deville, who suggested the title, and Ginny Weber, who explained antique keys and locks. I've always been pals with librarians, and this paid off with help from my son, John C. Sandstrom; from Holland, Michigan, librarian Robin Williams-Voight; and from two members of the Lunch Bunch, Susanna Fennema and Frantzie Couch. As usual, I also called on Michigan friends and neighbors Susan McDermott, Tracy Paquin, Judy Hallisy, and Dick Trull. Thanks also go to Ted Riley, who with a generous donation to the Lawton Arts for All campaign purchased the right for the name Rhonda Ringer-Riley to be used for a character in this book.

Chapter 1

Every native-born citizen of Warner Pier, Michigan, can diagram sentences. At least those over the age of twenty can.

This is because of the untiring efforts of the two Miss Ann Vanderklomps—aunt and niece—who between them taught English at Warner Pier High School over a period of sixty years. As a result of their work, everybody—*everybody*—who went to WPHS during that time period knows what it is to parse and how to do it.

This ability is not confined to those who have a literary bent. It is also held by people such as Tony Herrera, who has worked as a machinist ever since he finished high school, and whom I've never seen read a book. Tony has been one of my husband's best friends since their days on the WPHS wrestling team. Then around two years ago Tony's dad married my mother-in-law, so he and Joe—my husband—are now officially brothers.

Tony is intelligent, with a wonderful personality and top-notch mechanical skills, but when it comes to books, he waits for the movie version.

I was thinking this as Tony stood in the center of our living room. He held his nose, giving his voice a nasal tone, and at the same time he made that voice deep and dramatic. "The misplaced phrase is a bugaboo of the English language," he said. "Be ever on guard against it. Why, only last week there was a reference in the newspaper—the newspaper!—to a dog who, and I quote, 'returned to the inn where he and his master had been staying before going cross-country skiing.'"

Tony rolled his eyes dramatically and adjusted imaginary bra straps. Then he picked up his bottle of Labatt Blue beer and pretended to use a straw to drink from it, slurping rudely. His audience—all five of us— laughed loudly.

"That prepositional phrase is completely misplaced," Tony said, putting the beer down. "It should have been at the beginning of the sentence. That would make it clear"—he shook his right forefinger, but pinched his nose with his left hand—"it was the dog, not his master, who went cross-country skiing."

We all continued laughing as Tony released his grip on his nose. He spoke in his normal baritone. "Lee, you're gonna love getting to know Miss Vanderklomp." Then he dropped back into his seat on our couch and took a normal swig of Labatt Blue. "And don't let that water bottle she carries everywhere fool you. It's not water. It's Pepsi. She'd kill a kid who brought a soda to class, but she's never without her Pepsi."

The six of us, all early thirtyish, were having dinner at our house on a late September evening. Three of the group—Joe, Tony, and Tony's wife, Lindy—had grown up in this small Lake Michigan resort town and were

Warner Pier High School grads. Two others, Maggie and Ken McNutt, had moved to Warner Pier five years earlier and both taught at that high school. I'm Lee Woodyard, and I came to Warner Pier from my native Texas to become business manager for TenHuis Chocolade, the luxury chocolate shop my Aunt Nettie owns.

All six of us are firmly entrenched in the life of our little town, and Lindy, Tony, Joe, and I have a complicated series of interconnected relationships. Mike Herrera, Tony's dad and Joe's stepfather, owns two Warner Pier restaurants and a catering service, and has served as mayor of Warner Pier (population: 2,500) for three terms. Not only have Joe and Tony been pals since high school, but Lindy and I worked in the retail shop at TenHuis Chocolade when we were both sixteen. Several years ago Tony's dad, Mayor Mike, hired Joe as city attorney. Then Joe's mom married Mike, and Joe quit his city job to avoid any appearance of nepotism. And Lindy works for her father-in-law's company, managing one of his restaurants and running the catering operation.

When you throw in the fact that my aunt—who, as owner of TenHuis Chocolade, is my boss—married the Warner Pier police chief, well, a normal mind would be boggled. If you drew a diagram of our relationships, it would look like a genealogy of some European royal family in which cousins routinely married cousins.

Maggie and Ken were the only normal people present.

Tony's imitation of the fabled Miss Vanderklomp had been inspired by my mentioning that I'd been asked to serve on the Warner Pier library board. Miss Vanderklomp was active in that group.

"Aw, c'mon," I said. "I've never actually met her, but I'm sure Miss Vanderklomp can't be that bad. She's funny-looking, true, since she does her hair like a Dutch boy, and she's got that husky Dutch-boy build. She can't help looking as if she's ready to plug a finger in a dike."

"It's not anything to do with Miss Vanderklomp's appearance," Tony said. "She's just a character. Unforgettable. And unstoppable. You'll learn! Once she tells the board what the library is supposed to do, you might as well vote yea. She's going to get her own way."

"Yeah," Joe said. "That's the way she taught English, and that's the way she runs the library board."

"She can't run the board," I said. "She's not even a member. She doesn't have a vote." I turned to Maggie and Ken. "How do y'all know her? Neither of you went to high school here, and she retired before you joined the faculty."

"Oh, Miss Vanderklomp drops by to meet the new teachers every fall," Ken said.

Maggie groaned. "Thank goodness I don't teach English. She's a force of nature when it comes to the school. And it's just the way Tony says—she makes her wishes known. And her wishes do not include the teaching, or even the reading, of certain books."

"Oh, golly! Is she a censor? Ready to throw out *Catcher in the Rye* because the teenager in it thinks about sex?"

Everybody but me shook their heads. "No," Lindy said. "*Catcher in the Rye* doesn't bother her. It has 'literary merit.' But woe to the girl who gets caught reading a romance novel in the cafeteria. The way I did. I got a public lecture on my lowbrow taste."

"Yep," Maggie said. "One of the new English teachers told the sophomores they could pick anything they wanted for a book report. When Miss Vanderklomp heard that someone had done a Star Wars novel, she had the poor teacher in tears for permitting such a thing."

At that point I heard the timer go off in the kitchen. I stood up. "Dinner is ready. Joe, you see if anybody needs a drink refill, and I'll get the chicken Tetrazzini."

Lindy followed me into the kitchen. "Anyway, Lee, you're going on the library board at an interesting time."

"Because of the new building, you mean?"

"Yes, and the new director. I met him Tuesday, and I don't think he's going to kowtow to Miss Vanderklomp and her buddies on the board. You may be in a fight over the selection of books pretty quick."

"A fight? Over the books? I don't plan on that. When they ask an accountant to join a board, they usually want somebody to look at the finances. Of course, the city handles the library's finances, since this is just an advisory board."

"Plus Carol Turley is on the board, and she's treasurer of everything in town."

"I think she's secretary-treasurer of this board. That probably means the treasurer's job is minor."

"But who asked you to serve?"

"Jim Plaidy was the one who called."

"The vice mayor?"

"It's a city appointment. Look, Lindy, I thought it was a routine request. I just went off the chamber of commerce board, so I told Jim I'd think about accepting a new chore. The only complication is that I also got asked to join the tourism committee at the chamber, and I don't want to take two new jobs at the same time. But you know the drill. If you're going to live in a town like Warner Pier, you have to do what you can to keep the community functioning."

"True. We're not large enough to have a village id-

iot . . ." Lindy let her voice trail off, and I finished her
sentence.

"So we all have to take turns."

We both grinned at the old joke. I took the chicken
Tetrazzini out of the oven. Lindy grabbed the beet
salad, and we served up dinner. I forgot about Lindy's
warning.

Or maybe I didn't. Something I can't explain made
me delay accepting the appointment to the library
board. I decided I'd attend a meeting before I agreed to
join the body.

Finding a body? That never crossed my mind.

Chapter 2

The library board meetings were held at seven o'clock on the second Monday of the month in the meeting room at the library. The October meeting was to be the final one held in the old library. And believe me, "old" was an accurate word for that building.

In fact, the library building was one of the oldest in Warner Pier, and Warner Pier was founded in the 1840s. The structure's history had been traced in a recent article in the *Warner Pier Weekly Gazette*, and the information was fresh in my mind.

The library was housed in a two-story frame building that originally held a store downstairs and living quarters for the store's owner upstairs. A man named Andreas Vanderklomp built the building, and generations of Vanderklomps ran the store and lived above it.

But the Vanderklomps had a tradition that was more than commercial. From the earliest days, according to the article, at least one daughter in each generation had become a teacher.

The early-day Miss Vanderklomps had taught in one-room schoolhouses, of course. After Warner Pier opened a high school, the Miss Vanderklomps taught there. Miss Emily Vanderklomp taught mathematics beginning in 1928. And in 1945, the first Miss Ann Vanderklomp had been hired to teach English. In 1975 she had been joined by a niece, another Miss Ann Vanderklomp, who also taught English. For ten years they overlapped, and any confusion was avoided by the use of initials. The older Miss Vanderklomp was N. Ann Vanderklomp, and the younger one—the one who now haunted the library board—was G. Ann Vanderklomp.

Around about 1950, the Vanderklomp store closed. In fact, I think the Miss Vanderklomp Tony had parodied is today the last member of the family living in Warner Pier. And when the store closed, the owners—the brother of Miss N. Ann and the parents of Miss G. Ann—donated the building to the city for use as a library. They also donated the family's book collection, and when browsing the shelves of the Warner Pier Public Library today it's still possible to run across a 1944 Book of the Month Club selection with a Vanderklomp bookplate inside the front cover.

Gradually the old building deteriorated. Today the upstairs floor sags, and the whole building needs to be rewired. Just after I moved to Warner Pier four years ago, a bond referendum approved construction of a new library. That building, near Warner Pier High School, was now nearly completed and was scheduled to open in a month. As Lindy had mentioned, the library also had a new director, a man named Henry Cassidy. His nickname, or so I'd read in the *Gazette*, was Butch, and he was forty-two. I hadn't met him yet.

Like all meetings of city committees, the library

board meetings are open to the public unless certain subjects are being discussed, so I didn't wait for a special invitation. I trailed into the library at about ten to seven on the appointed day. The library closes at seven on Mondays, so the few patrons left were lining up to check out their selections. A plump, middle-aged woman was staffing the front desk—her name plate read BETTY BLAKE, ASSISTANT LIBRARIAN—and she stopped checking out books long enough to direct me to the meeting and tell me to feel free to look around.

Following her instructions, I walked a long way down a narrow passage between towering shelves; the library is one of those long, narrow buildings that seem to go on forever. I passed the broad public stairs that lead to the second floor, where the reference and nonfiction sections are. A narrower set of stairs, or so I'd been told, was available at the back of the building. I went past the rolling ladders along the walls, now tied down for safety reasons, and I identified the inconspicuous door—marked STAFF ONLY—that led to the workroom. I peeked inside and found a typical cluttered space. Next came another door. Looking inside, I discovered a tiny hall with access to the back door leading to the alley and to the back stairs leading up, as well as to the basement stairs going down.

Near that door was a little room with a beat-up metal table in the middle. A dozen folding chairs with lightly padded seats were lined up along the walls. I'd found the meeting room.

When I entered the tiny room, one person was already there: Dr. Albert Cornwall, a retired history professor I had met a few times. Dr. Cornwall's friends called him Corny. I called him Dr. Cornwall.

Dr. Cornwall was sitting in the corner, with his chair tipped back against the wall in a pose that looked quite precarious. I was tempted to clap my hands, whistle, or make some other startling noise, to see if he'd fall over. Of course, I resisted that impulse. If Dr. Cornwall fell over, he'd probably break a hip. I guessed his age at early eighties, maybe late eighties.

Dr. Cornwall was dozing. Dr. Cornwall was often dozing these days.

I picked up an agenda from a stack at the end of the meeting table and sat down quietly, since I didn't want to be the one who disturbed him. I'd barely seated myself when we were joined by Rhonda Ringer-Riley, the board chair. Mrs. Ringer-Riley was sixtyish, with blond hair in one of the tones considered suitable for older ladies. She wore a coordinated sportswear outfit, and she carried a large flowered tote bag.

Rhonda, I knew, was a local. As a resort town, Warner Pier has three classes of society: tourists, summer people, and locals. Locals, like Rhonda and me, live here year-round; tourists stay only a few days, and summer people own or lease property and spend longer periods of time here, but vote elsewhere. Dr. Cornwall represented a new and growing class—summer people who have retired to Warner Pier. They're not quite local; it takes several winters before they move beyond their summer-resident status. But they're becoming a force in the town.

Rhonda had inherited a half dozen lakeshore tourist cottages, and she and her husband rented them out each summer, so they were part of the Warner Pier business community. Their cottages and their home were about a mile from where Joe and I lived, south along the shore of Lake Michigan.

"Oh, hi, Lee," she said. "I heard that you're to replace Abigail on the board."

"I'm not sure yet."

"You should take the job. There's nothing to it but one meeting a month."

"I would have thought you'd have been quite busy for the past year, what with the planning and construction of the new building."

"The director—the former director, Catherine Smith—took care of nearly everything. We're a rubber-stamp body, I'm afraid." Was her tone a bit on the dry side? Or was that my imagination?

Rhonda sat down and produced a notebook and pen from her tote bag. She laid these on the table; then she took out a large piece of knitting.

Before I could question her about the board, a tall, slender young woman came in. She had long brown hair and carried a baby in a sling. At the door to the room she turned back and spoke firmly. "Geraldine, you're to keep an eye on Hal. Stay strictly in the children's section. Any problems, come and get me."

I recognized her, too. Gwen Swain. She was the wife of an engineer who worked at a power plant south of us. Lindy called her the Earth Mother. I knew from Lindy that Gwen homeschooled her oldest child and had been known to nurse her baby while browsing the produce at the Superette. For the moment the baby was napping.

Gwen gave me a vigorous handshake and sat down next to Dr. Cornwall.

Hard on her heels, Carol Turley stomped in with her usual awkward gait. She carried a fancy red leather folder, a sort of miniature briefcase.

Gwen spoke to her. "Oh, hi, Carol. Is that the case you were telling me about?"

"Yes," she said, and smiled a rather nervous smile. But she blinked her eyes so rapidly I thought she was trying not to cry. "Yes, Brian gave it to me last week. For my birthday."

"That was a sweet thing to do," Gwen said.

Carol blinked harder. "Yes, my husband really is a sweetie."

Maybe so, I thought, but he's not real romantic. I mean, a leather folder isn't a diamond ring or even a dozen roses. But I guess it was something Carol would use all the time.

Carol dropped the folder on the table, and it made quite a thud. Dr. Cornwall jumped and opened his eyes. Luckily, his chair did not go over.

Carol was the kind of person who is never noticed in a crowd. She was about my age and short, with dull blond hair. But I couldn't call Carol plain; her big brown eyes were too expressive. She shut them tightly, then popped them open. After taking a deep breath, she spoke to me. Her voice had its usual whine. "I see you've decided to join us."

"Actually, this is an exploratory visit," I said.

"Well, there's nothing to it," Carol said. She twisted her hands together nervously. "Between the library director and the city engineer, we have strong guidance. There's never any question of how to vote."

"But you're getting a new library director," I said. "He may expect more participation from the board."

"Why?" Now Carol's voice was not only loud, but also incredulous. "We just stand back and stay out of the way. Unless he pulls some dumb stunt."

"And I'll try not to do that."

A bass voice sounded from the doorway, and we all turned to look at a person who was designed by nature to be called Butch. He was tall—maybe six-three—and rough-hewn, with a large, blocky build, and a friendly grin. But the most eye-catching thing about him was a gorgeous streak of gray at each temple. He looked like an ad for men's hair color. If I owned such a company

I would have made him our official spokesman on the spot.

"I'm sure you've all figured out that I'm Butch Cassidy," he said. "And I'd appreciate it if you'd tell me who you are."

He walked around the table and shook hands with each of us.

I was the final person he greeted, so I had a minute to take him in.

Sexy. He was sexy. My innards noticed that right away.

By the time he reached my side of the table, "sexy" was definitely the word I'd picked to describe him. It wasn't that he was particularly handsome; Joe was a lot better-looking. Butch just seemed to broadcast sex appeal.

All the women seemed to grow more feminine as he spoke to them. The prim Rhonda Ringer-Riley almost simpered. Gwen looked more Earth Motherish. Carol Turley even managed not to say anything else rude. "I'm Carol Turley," she said. "I'm secretary-treasurer." Then she sat down abruptly, almost missing her chair.

But the stupid comment was left for me. I extended my hand to the new director and said, "I'm Lee McKinney. I mean, Woodwind. I mean, Woodyard. Lee Woodyard. And I'm not a member of the body. Board."

I quit then. I had completely messed up, and I had the sense to know things might get even worse. I'm famous for my twisted tongue, but I'd outdone myself.

Rhonda looked pained, and Carol Turley giggled. "Well, who are you, Lee?" She giggled again.

Butch—I was already thinking of him by that name—ignored Carol. "Guests are always welcome," he said. He sat down next to Rhonda. "We seem to have a quorum, Mrs. Ringer-Riley. Shall we start?"

Rhonda looked surprised. "Oh. But Miss Vanderklomp isn't here yet."

Butch consulted a paper. "Vanderklomp? Is she a member of the board?"

"No. No, she's an honorary member. She always attends. It seems—well, rude to start without her."

Butch frowned.

"And she's here!"

Miss Vanderklomp shot into the room as if she'd been propelled by a cannon. "Late, as usual!" Her voice was close to a shout, and, yes, it managed to be both nasal and very deep. She was tall, nearly as tall as I am, and I'm close to six feet. Her build was husky, and her silver-gray hair was cropped into a thick Dutch bob that stuck out over each ear. She dropped several file folders and a plastic water bottle onto the table. She plunked herself into a folding chair with such force I expected the chair to collapse. She reached inside her blouse—first the right shoulder, then the left—and adjusted her bra straps. Then she took a drink from her water bottle. It was the opaque kind of plastic, so you couldn't see the color of its contents. It could well have held Pepsi, just as Tony had claimed.

"Sorry for my dilatory habits," she boomed.

I was staring openmouthed. Tony's parody of her had been unbelievably accurate. For the first time I fully appreciated his humor.

But nobody on the library board laughed.

Instead, Gwen spoke quietly. "Abigail Montgomery isn't here either."

"She's in the building," Rhonda said. "I saw her when I came in. She'll be along. Let the meeting come to order."

Apparently no one was concerned about waiting for Abigail, even though Abigail, unlike Miss Vanderklomp, was an official member of the board. In fact, she was the person I had been invited to replace. That seemed rather odd.

The meeting went on. Abigail didn't appear. No one seemed to notice.

The business seemed routine. Minutes, various committees. There was a simple financial report from Butch Cassidy. This made me ask about Carol's duties as secretary-treasurer, and Carol explained that the title "treasurer" simply indicated she chaired the financial committee. A library staff member kept any financial records, passing them on to the city treasurer.

After twenty minutes I had concluded that Carol's assessment of the board was right; they didn't do much.

Actually, there was not much need for them to take action. The staff and building expenses for the library were paid by the Village of Warner Pier. The city council, for example, had officially hired the new director. The board merely advised on programs and operations. They were more citizen representatives than officials.

Butch Cassidy didn't suggest any revolutionary changes at his first meeting. His report didn't draw much reaction until he got to the final item.

"I found a request for a change in hours among the director's files," he said. "I was surprised to learn that the Warner Pier Public Library has never been open on Sundays."

"The previous director didn't recommend that," Rhonda said.

"In August a group of students requested that the library be open Sunday afternoons during the school year. This seems to be a reasonable request, and I've—"

"Humph!" The syllable exploded from Miss Vanderklomp's lips. "Think carefully, Mr. Cassidy! That might be a dangerous precedent!"

Butch looked surprised. Then he frowned. "But it's standard practice—"

He didn't get to finish his sentence. Before he could say another word, an enormous shriek echoed through the building.

We all reacted. I jumped up and headed for the door. Gwen's baby joined the clamor. The front legs of Dr. Cornwall's chair hit the floor with a crash. Carol yelled out, "What's that? What! What!"

I was the first person out, because I'd been nearest the door. The noise was coming from across the main room. Peering between the stacks, I saw Betty Blake, the clerk who'd been checking out books, running toward the front of the building.

I scurried after her. "What's wrong? What's wrong?"

"Help! Call 9-1-1!"

"What's happened?"

"I think it's Abigail! Abigail Montgomery! She's in a heap at the bottom of the basement stairs. She's not breathing!"

She cried out again. "She's dead! She's dead! Call someone!"

Chapter 3

There was a mad rush to the tiny back hall and then to the basement door. Since I'd been the first one out of the room, I was the first one down the stairs, and Butch was right behind me. The others hovered at the top of the steps.

The light was poor, but when Butch and I knelt over Abigail Montgomery, I felt sure she was dead. She was lying on her stomach, with her head turned slightly to the side. Blood from a wound on the back of her head had made a puddle on the floor. I couldn't find a pulse, and when Butch held a scrap of paper in front of her nose, it didn't give a quiver. She wasn't breathing.

"She's gone," Butch said.

He called out to the group at the top of the stairs. "Please go back to the boardroom. I'll call 9-1-1 on my cell phone. Then I'll wait for the EMTs at the front door."

Everybody moved back except Miss Vanderklomp.

She came down two steps and growled a comment. "It doesn't seem right to leave her alone."

Butch went up the stairs and edged past her. "I think it will be okay."

"I feel that someone should stay with her."

The darn woman was bossing just for the sake of bossing. I felt really annoyed.

"It's all right, Miss Vanderklomp," I said. I spoke as firmly as I could, considering that my insides were sloshing around like Lake Michigan on a windy day. "I'll stay here."

I followed Butch partway up the stairs and sat down, firmly planting my fanny on a step, then spreading my arms and legs out so that Miss Vanderklomp would have to jump over me if she tried to come farther.

"I could stay," she said.

"Oh, I have completed first-aid training," I said.

Which was true, but had nothing to do with anything. First aid was not going to help Abigail Montgomery.

The comment did make Miss Vanderklomp pause, although she was still lingering on the step, frowning.

"Plus," I said, "I'm sure you know the chief of police is married to my aunt."

That shut her up, even though that circumstance also had nothing to do with anything. She sniffed irately and went back upstairs. At least she left the door open. I didn't want to be down there alone with what had been Abigail.

Not that I was deeply grieved. In fact, although Abigail Montgomery had been pointed out to me, I didn't think I had ever spoken with her. My impression was that she led a rather reclusive life. I racked my brain, trying to remember what I knew or had heard about her.

Abigail was a member of a fairly prominent family in Warner Pier. They had also been prominent in both Michigan state affairs and in Chicago. They had "cottaged" in Warner Pier since forever, and Abigail was one of those summer people who had come to live in Warner Pier after she retired, moving to a home she and her husband had built years earlier at the family compound.

Abigail's maiden name had been Hart, and the Hart family had a few skeletons in their closets that I already knew about. Her brother, Timothy Hart, is one of the sweetest men I know—he helped save my life once upon a time—but he's a chronic alcoholic. Her sister . . . Well, the less said about her sister, the better. Her brother-in-law had a strange life, as well as a strange death. However, her nephew, Hart VanHorn, is a former Michigan state legislator who is now a leading lawyer in Grand Rapids, and as far as I know is a perfectly nice guy.

I knew nothing about Mr. Montgomery, whoever he had been, but Abigail had lived in California for many years. I had a vague impression, drawn from Warner Pier gossip, that she had moved back to the family compound for financial reasons. She'd been a year-round resident for three or four years, and since my father-in-law is the mayor, I happened to hear that Hart called him and asked him to find his aunt some sort of committee to serve on. "She needs to get out more," her nephew said, "and she could make a genuine contribution to the community." "She's incredibly shy," Hart had said, "but she's an intelligent and well-read woman."

"Well read." Aha. Mike had named her to the library board, and she had served two years. Abigail was declining a second term because she'd developed health problems.

I rapidly reviewed this information as I waited for the EMTs. But nothing that I had ever heard about Abigail Montgomery told me what I'd really like to know: What the heck had she been doing falling down the basement stairs in the Warner Pier Public Library when she should have been up in the meeting room?

I looked around that basement. Only the area around the bottom of the stairs was illuminated. A bare bulb swung above my head, but the light it gave left parts of the room too glary and other parts too shadowy. The basement extended off into the dim, dark recesses of the building. I guessed that it was the same size as the upstairs, but I certainly couldn't tell for sure.

What I could see were bare wooden stairs—the kind with empty space between the treads—and I was sitting on those. There were heaps of boxes, tables loaded with books, and an old rack that must have once held newspapers. The area was cool, too, and the air had a damp, cellarlike feeling.

By the time I heard heavy footsteps thumping over my head and realized that Authority of some sort had arrived, I was definitely ready to get out of that basement. But, of course, I couldn't. Butch and the Warner Pier PD's night patrolman came down the stairs, and I couldn't get past them. Instead I had to get up and move farther into the basement to let them in. The EMT crew was right behind them. I had to move even farther into the basement to let that group have room. So I wound up standing about twenty feet away, behind a table, while all the men blocked the steps that would have allowed me to escape. There was nothing I could do but wait.

And look around. I admit I did that. I didn't want to

watch the undignified things that were being done to Abigail, so I looked elsewhere.

After my eyes adjusted to the dark I did find another hanging lightbulb, the kind with a pull chain. So I pulled it on. That illuminated a new area of the spooky basement. Not that there was much to see. It was more of the same. Broken chairs, a heap of boards that might once have been a bookshelf, and stacks of old books.

The most interesting item was that old rack that had once held newspapers. People younger than I am might never have seen one, now that library patrons access old newspapers by computer. But when my grandmother took the five-year-old me to the children's story hour at the library back in Prairie Creek, Texas, that library had a special rack for newspapers.

It's hard to describe; the only thing similar I've ever seen might be a folding drying rack. Wooden sticks hung on staggered pegs, and newspapers hung on the sticks. They were staggered so that the newspapers in front wouldn't block access to the newspapers in back. The back of the rack stood about five feet from the floor, and the front row of pegs about three feet. The wooden rods had some sort of clamps or slots to hold the newspapers.

The racks I had grown up with had metal rods, but this rack had wooden rods to hold each type of newspaper. There were a half dozen sets of pegs to hold the rods. The rack had probably once held recent issues of the *Warner Pier Weekly Gazette*, the *Holland Sentinel*, the *Grand Rapids Press*, and the *Chicago Tribune*. Probably the *Chicago Sun*, too, back then, when major cities had more than one daily.

Because I didn't want to think about the work going on with Abigail, I found myself wondering whether the library had originally bought the rack secondhand. The wooden rods were surely older than the metal rods I remembered.

Five empty wooden rods were lined up on the old rack, but one set of pegs was empty. Then I saw the extra rod. It was on the floor between me and the group of emergency workers kneeling near the stairs.

I went over and picked it up. The basement was a mess, but at least I could do one little thing to neaten it up.

As I turned toward the rack, something on the wooden rod I was holding caught my eye. Hair. A clump of hair was sticking to the thick end of the rod. That seemed odd. I pulled it close to my eyes, trying to see it in the harsh light. And I saw that a crack ran down one side of the rod, a crack that wasn't supposed to be there.

At that moment Hogan Jones came in. My aunt's husband. Warner Pier police chief. An experienced detective from a big city who had moved to Warner Pier and taken on the job of police chief as a retirement activity.

Hogan stopped about halfway down the stairs and spoke to the EMTs. "Accident?"

One of the EMTs stood up. "I don't know, Hogan. She seems to have fallen forward, but there's a depression at the base of her skull. To tell you the truth—and I'm no expert—I think you'll want an autopsy. It looks like the traditional blunt instrument to me."

I took one more look at the wooden rod I was holding. Hair. It had hair on it. And it had a crack running down the side. As if it had hit something. Hard. Suddenly it seemed to be burning hot. I dropped it back on the basement floor, and it made quite a clatter. Everyone stared at me.

I looked at Hogan, then at the rod. Could the long wooden piece be a murder weapon? It wasn't very big around, nothing like a baseball bat. I looked back at Hogan and put my hands behind my back, like a naughty child caught at the cookie jar. Then I pulled them out and gestured toward the rod. The EMTs, the police, even Butch—all of them were still staring at me.

"Sorry to make such a clobber—I mean, a clatter!" I said. "I just realized that stick has a long crack down the side. And it seems to have hair on it. And maybe . . . something else."

Every jaw in the room dropped. Except Hogan's. The dadgum man never loses his aplomb.

"Lee," he said, "what are you doing hanging around a crime scene?"

"Hogan, I didn't know it was a crime scene until"—I gestured toward the EMT who had spoken—"until that guy said . . . what he said. I thought it was an accident scene. And I would have left, except that everybody blocked the stairs and I couldn't get out!"

Hogan nodded. "I see your problem." He turned sideways and motioned to his patrolman. "Jerry, you step aside and let Lee get to the stairs. And, Mr. Cassidy, you can leave now, too."

The silence grew as I walked across to the stairs and started up. Butch came close behind me. As we edged by, Hogan blocked our way with one hand.

"I'm sure I can count on both of you to keep your mouths shut about Pete's remark."

Pete? For a moment I felt quite blank. Then I realized Pete must be the EMT who had spoken, saying Abigail had a depression at the base of her skull. I nodded, agreeing to keep quiet.

Then I leaned close to Hogan. "I hope I didn't spoil the fenderprints—fingerprints!—when I picked up that rod. I was just being neat."

"Not your fault, Lee." Hogan dropped his hand, and Butch and I went on upstairs.

My mind was racing. But I didn't believe what I'd just heard. It just didn't seem possible that someone had killed Abigail Montgomery. Why on earth would anyone do that? She sounded like the most inoffensive person who ever lived. Her nephew had described her as shy.

Not that shy people don't get killed. But usually it's us brash types who inspire the blunt-instrument treatment.

Butch and I went to the meeting room. The board members, plus Betty Blake, were sitting around the table, looking solemn. The exception might have been Miss Vanderklomp. She wasn't looking shy. She was looking efficient and bossy, but I doubt she had any other expression.

"I called Timothy Hart," she said smugly.

Butch looked blank. "Who is Timothy Hart?"

"Mrs. Montgomery's brother. I've never met him, but I thought the family should be informed."

I started to remark that Hogan might have liked to give Tim the news himself, but before the words were out of my mouth I realized they were pointless.

"Was Tim alone?" I said.

"As far as I know. Why?"

"Because Tim doesn't drive. I'll call my husband and ask him to bring Tim down. He lives only a quarter of a mile from us."

I called the house, but Joe didn't answer, so I tried his cell phone. His voice didn't sound too happy.

"Joe, could you give Timothy Hart a ride down to the library? I can't leave here to pick him up."

"We're on our way. Tim already called me."

"Good. How's he doing?"

"About the usual."

"Uh-oh."

"Yeah. We'll be there in five minutes."

My "uh-oh" had reflected our knowledge that the usual for Tim meant he'd been drinking. He's a sweet guy, drunk or sober, but after five or six strong drinks over a couple of hours he doesn't track any better than any of us would with that blood-alcohol level.

As soon as I hung up, Miss Vanderklomp spoke. "I thought Timothy Hart lived out on Lake Shore Drive."

"That's right."

"How does he manage, if he doesn't know how to drive?"

I hesitated, because I didn't know what to say, but Carol Turley jumped right in there. "He knows. He lost his license after his third DUI," she said.

Miss Vanderklomp raised her eyebrows. I guess I glared at Carol, because she spoke defensively. "Well, it's true!"

I turned to Miss Vanderklomp. "Tim has a lot of problems," I said, "but he's a nice person, and he's been a good neighbor to us." Then I looked all around the room, making sure Carol got part of the look. "Joe said he and Tim will be here within five minutes."

Carol had the grace to look embarrassed.

And, sure enough, almost immediately I heard Joe's voice, and when I looked out the door of the meeting room, I saw a cop escorting Tim and Joe toward us. "You'll have to wait until the chief can get loose," the cop told them.

I greeted Tim with a big hug. He looked as if he was about to cry. "Lee, is it true? Is Abby really dead?"

"I'm afraid so, Tim."

Tears did well up in his eyes then. He shook his head sadly and spoke.

"Now I'll never know what she was so worried about."

Chapter 4

Abigail Montgomery had been worried, but she hadn't told her brother what she had been worried about.

Darn! That information could well have been the number-one clue to who killed her. But the silly woman hadn't shared her secret.

I wanted to quiz Tim, but I kept my mouth shut. After all, it was Hogan who would ask the official questions, and he was an expert. No matter how nosy I was, I should keep out of it. I confined my activities to taking Tim by the arm and leading him into the room where we were all waiting. Apparently that was the place where the investigators wanted to corral noninvestigators. The tiny room was getting crowded.

Several of the waiting board members made consoling remarks to Tim. Rhonda Ringer-Riley gave him a hug. Butch found two more of the uncomfortable chairs for Tim and for Joe, and we all sat down to wait.

It was Carol who offered to make coffee. She's always

full of surprises. After her unkind remarks about Tim's driving, she gave him a particularly sweet greeting. She seemed genuinely interested in trying to comfort him.

Our guardian cop allowed her to go back to the workroom, where library employees took their breaks. After ten minutes or so she brought back a carafe of coffee and some Styrofoam cups, and Butch found a sack of bargain chocolate chip cookies someplace. I hadn't felt particularly hungry, but never have Hills Bros. coffee and store-bought cookies tasted so good. I guess we were all in need of comfort.

Even Tim had some coffee, though he refused a cookie. The coffee seemed to help him. His talk grew less confused, and his eyes almost focused.

The aroma of coffee may have reminded Hogan that we were there, because he almost immediately came upstairs. He took Tim away.

I could hear Tim talking as they walked off. "I'm afraid the Harts have become a doomed family," he said. "This is the third violent death for my generation. Now I'm the only one left."

"You've sure had a run of bad luck," Hogan said kindly. "Have you called Hart to tell him about his aunt?" Then they were out of earshot.

Back in the meeting room, Rhonda seemed to reassume her job as chair. "Tim's right," she said. "A lot has happened to the Hart family in the past few years. But I never expected the bad luck to move on to Abigail. She was always the quiet one."

"Had you known her for a long time?" I asked.

"Our mothers were friends. Abby was a nice little girl—docile. Not assertive. Nothing like her sister."

Miss Vanderklomp cleared her throat, adjusted her bra straps, and spoke. "These people—these Harts— they didn't go to school in Warner Pier, did they?"

"No," Rhonda said. "They were from Chicago. All three of the children went to private school there."

"Then how did you meet them?"

"Their cottage was near our house. Their mother was very nice. She and my mother had known each other when they played on the beach as kids."

"I see." Miss Vanderklomp picked up her water—or was it Pepsi?—bottle and pulled on the straw. Her body language spoke volumes. If this Hart family hadn't gone to Warner Pier High School, they hadn't existed for Miss Vanderklomp.

I turned to Rhonda. "Then you knew them well."

Rhonda nodded. "Olivia was the bossy one. Hart's mother."

She and I exchanged looks. I could testify to how bossy Olivia was. But I didn't say anything about Olivia. I wanted to keep the focus on Abigail. "Whom did Abigail marry?"

"Bill Montgomery. He was from another summer family. He was in Vietnam when they got married—I mean, he was just back. They built a house on the Hart property, but they didn't use it for years. Bill went to work for the family bank. In Chicago. Then he went to work for a bank in California." Rhonda shrugged, and I had the feeling Bill had never progressed much as a banker.

"Abigail came back here after he died," she said. "I called and asked her to go out to lunch several times, but she wasn't very social. I mostly saw her here at the board meetings."

Rhonda blinked, looking almost as if she were going to burst into tears. "She was such a mild-mannered person."

A loud grunting noise sounded, and I jumped all over. I wondered if we had a hog or some other kind of animal in the room. But when I turned toward the noise, it was Dr. Cornwall.

His eyes were wide open, and he was glaring at Rhonda. "You make Abigail sound like a sort of angel," he said in a gruff voice. "She wasn't."

"Corny!" Rhonda sounded scandalized.

"You're trying to observe the conventions, avoid speaking ill of the dead. But we all know your description of Abigail isn't the whole picture. We were all here when she let Carol have it at last month's meeting. And we heard the discussion when she and Gwen bumped heads over the air-conditioning in the new building. And when those things happened, Abigail held up her end of the argument! People didn't trample Abigail Montgomery into the ground. No, they didn't! Abigail had that Hart spirit! She could stare down her nose with the best of them!"

Carol made a noise. I expected her to follow Dr. Cornwall's comments by saying something. I guess everybody else did, too, because we all turned and looked at her. But she didn't say anything more. She simply sank into her chair, looking crushed.

We sat quietly and sipped our coffee. Even Rhonda didn't argue with the opposing view of Abigail Montgomery.

It was then I noticed that Gwen was gone. Rhonda said that Hogan had let her go home, since she had all three of her children with her. "I really don't see why any of us have to stay," she said. "I mean, just because of an accident. None of us even saw it."

I glanced at Butch and discovered he was looking at me. I moved nervously and even felt my face grow warm. But neither of us said anything about Abigail's death not being an accident.

We didn't have to stay too long after that. Hogan

escorted Tim back and took quick statements from each of us—basically asking what time we arrived and whether we'd seen Abigail Montgomery before we went in for the meeting. Then he said we could leave. He also told Tim he could go. The older man left with Joe and me. I almost got into Joe's truck before I realized I had come in my own van.

By then I was feeling a new concern for Tim. "Tim, have you had anything to eat?"

"I'm not hungry."

Joe and I exchanged looks. We were both reared with the belief that missing a meal might ruin our health forever. Plus, food might counteract the amount of alcohol Tim had taken in earlier.

"Lee and I were planning to stop at Herrera's for a quick bite," Joe said. "Would you mind coming along?"

There was no way Tim could refuse, of course, since he was riding with Joe.

Herrera's is one of two restaurants owned by Joe's stepfather, Mike Herrera. It's the fancier one, which might not make it suitable for a grieving brother, but it's also the quieter. Plus, it was open. There are dozens of restaurants in Warner Pier, as befits a resort community, but a large proportion of them close from Labor Day until Memorial Day.

So Joe, Tim, and I went to Herrera's. Luckily, Mike Herrera himself was on duty, and I was able to explain the situation to him. He gave us his most secluded table. I twisted Tim's arm until he ordered a bowl of chicken and noodles and a small salad. Tim was sobering up fast, but getting some food down him could only help.

Tim didn't have a cell phone—"Can't seem to hang on to them," he said—but he had Hart's business card, and Joe was able to reach Hart halfway between Grand

Rapids and Warner Pier. Joe assured him we would take his uncle home. Hart said he'd stop by the library to check in with the authorities, then meet all of us at Tim's house.

We were just finishing our meal when Butch Cassidy walked in. He looked harassed, but still I noticed how attractive he was. We all waved, and he took a table across the room. In a few minutes the waitress placed a large martini in front of him.

Joe looked at it, then grinned at me. I grinned back. Both of us would have loved a drink, but we were not going to touch a drop in front of Tim.

Joe and Tim soon left, leaving me behind to sign the credit card slip. To my surprise, as soon as they were out the door Butch came over to the table.

"May I ask you a question, Mrs. Woodyard?"

"Of course. Sit down. And please call me Lee."

My words, I hoped, sounded routine. What weren't routine were the internal flutters I was feeling. I firmly reminded myself that I was a married woman—a happily married woman—and tried to put on a friendly expression. "How can I do you?" Yikes! "I mean, how can I help you?"

Butch Cassidy didn't laugh, but he blinked a couple of times.

I spoke again. "I'm the Mrs. Malaprop of Warner Pier. Just ignore my tongue." Oh, Lordy, I'd done it again! Everything I said seemed to have a double meaning. I put on a smile that I'm sure looked as twisted as my words. Then I shut up.

"When we were downstairs, after we found Mrs. Montgomery," Butch said, "did you say something about being related to the police chief?"

"We're what Texans call shirttail relations. My mother's brother was Chief Jones' wife's first husband." Butch looked suitably confused, so I went on. "In other words, my aunt is married to him."

"Then he's your uncle by marriage?"

"Actually, he's the second husband of my aunt by marriage. I recommend that you settle for 'shirttail relative.' Or I can draw you a family tree. But since I work for that aunt and we're all pals, it's a closer relationship than it might sound like. But we're not blood kin, as my Texas grandma would have said."

"You're talking about Chief Jones, the one I met tonight?"

"Right. Hogan Jones."

"He seems like a—well, a competent person."

"Oh, he is. Warner Pier is lucky to have him." I quickly sketched Hogan's career—more than twenty years with the Cincinnati Police Department, ending as chief of detectives. Then retirement to Warner Pier. Losing his first wife to cancer. Deciding to take on a new job as police chief in a small—very small—town where he had to handle everything from dealing with the city council to investigating major crimes. Hogan never commented on which activity was more difficult.

Butch nodded seriously. "I could tell he really knows what he's doing. But more detectives came in after you left."

"Probably the Michigan State Police. Part of their function is assisting small communities with major investigations. They do the lab work, for one thing."

Butch had brought his martini along, and now he sipped it, looking serious. "Sounds as if they're planning a full-scale investigation."

"I doubt they'll commit until a doctor gets a look at Mrs. Montgomery."

Butch stood up. "Thanks, Mrs. . . . Lee. It's good to know what to expect."

"I think you can expect to have the library full of investigators for several days."

"Yep. None of us will have a secret left. No matter how insignificant."

"Please don't worry about it, Butch. I'm sure you'll find Hogan— and the state police detectives—very easy to work with. They're always polite and businesslike."

He went back to his own table, leaving me to wonder why he looked as if he were facing a dire fate. Dadgum! He was one sexy dude. I couldn't help thinking it, and it made me ashamed of myself, even though I had tried to act as if I didn't notice his attraction.

I was taking a final sip of my coffee, waiting to sign the credit card slip, when my cell phone rang. I looked to see who it was before I answered.

"Hogan?"

"Lee, where are you?"

"I'm at Herrera's. We stopped for dinner, trying to get some food down Timothy Hart."

"I need to talk to you again."

"Sure. I was going home."

"Just come on back to the library. And I don't suppose you know where that Cassidy guy is."

"As a matter of fact, he's here, too."

"With you?"

"No, but he's right across the room. He hasn't had his dinner yet."

"I need both of you back here, Lee. Now."

Chocolate Chat

Chocolate may improve the memories of snails. According to news reports, researchers at the Hotchkiss Brain Institute at the University of Calgary discovered this when they tested the effects of a flavonoid called epicatechin on the creatures. They tested red wine and green tea, as well as chocolate.

The snails were placed in tanks that contained either normal water or water containing a small amount of chocolate. Some of the oxygen was removed from the water. This makes the snails extend their breathing tubes more often.

Each time the snails extended their breathing tubes, the researchers poked them with a stick. (I'm sure they gave the snails a gentle, loving tap.) After half an hour the snails were removed from the chocolate-flavored water.

Later the snails were placed back in the water and the scientists measured how often they extended their breathing tubes. The assumption: If the snails popped the tubes out less often than they had earlier, they were "remembering" that they might get a tap with a stick if they did so.

The snails that had been in the normal water remembered to hold their breath for only three hours. The snails from the chocolate water remembered for twenty-four to forty-eight hours.

The researchers concluded that the epicatechin improved the snails' memories. This might—might—mean that I could find my car keys if I ate a few Hershey's Kisses. Maybe.

Chapter 5

Hogan needed me, and he needed Butch?
Why both of us? Why either of us?

I called Joe's cell phone and told him I wouldn't meet him as quickly as I had planned. Then I signed the credit card slip and got up to leave. By then Butch was talking on his own cell phone. He was frowning. Hogan must have reached him.

I could see the library from the Herrera's parking lot. There were so many police cars over there that I didn't bother to move my van, and I just walked over. As I crossed the street an ambulance pulled away. Abigail must have started her journey to autopsy and, eventually, burial.

Jerry Cherry, one of Hogan's patrolmen, let me in the library and sent me back to the meeting room. There Hogan and one of the state police detectives, Lieutenant Larry Underwood, had their heads together.

Underwood is a youngish detective—he's been a lieutenant for only a year or so. He's square and blocky, with a buzz cut. I'd run into him a couple of times before. We weren't exactly buddies.

Underwood and Hogan were looking at some papers spread out on the table. Each paper was enclosed in a plastic envelope. They both looked serious as they greeted me.

"How can I help?" I asked.

Hogan spoke. "Lee, while you were waiting for the ambulance crew, did you touch Abigail Montgomery's body at all?"

"Good night, no! I sat on the stairs. I didn't go near her. Then. Earlier I felt her wrist, trying to find a pulse."

"Then you didn't move her body?"

"No. Why would I do that?"

Hogan held up one of the plastic-encased sheets of paper from the table. "Can you identify this object?"

I took the envelope from him and looked at the document inside. Centered at the top was my name and address.

"Huh?" I read on. "It's my résumé! Where did that come from?"

Hogan didn't answer.

I studied the résumé. It was, I saw, current—meaning it was a printout of one I had updated within the past month. Where had Hogan gotten it?

"Like most people," I said, "I keep my résumé in my computer. There's a copy at the office and also one on the laptop I use at home. This one is dated last month. I updated it at that time at the request of the vice mayor."

"Jim Plaidy?"

"Right. He called me to ask if I'd serve on the library board. I said I'd think about it. He asked for a copy of my résumé, and I looked it over, then e-mailed a copy to him. He could have made a dozen printouts, of course."

"If he wanted to take the nomination to the council, he probably did."

"Maybe. But so far I haven't agreed to serve."

Hogan nodded and picked up another plastic envelope. "What about this?"

I looked at the document inside the envelope. It was an envelope addressed to a Henry C. Dunlap. His address was a post office box in Lansing, Michigan.

"I never saw it before," I said.

Hogan nodded. "Okay. How about this?"

This time he held up a paper sack, and he dumped its contents out on the table. All it held was a wooden pencil of ghastly chartreuse green.

"Oh no! Are those things still haunting us? After three years?"

The chartreuse green pencils were imprinted with the name of Joe's boat-restoration business, Heritage Boats. Several years earlier Joe had taken a space at a boat show, and he had ordered five hundred pencils to hand out. He deliberately picked the most eye-catching color in the promotional company's catalog. But the color turned out to be so horrible he couldn't even give the pencils away. They wrote fine and had exceptionally good erasers, but they were so ugly no one wanted one. The last time I'd looked he still had four hundred of them on his desk at the boat shop.

But Joe has his economical side. He wouldn't just throw them out. So I had started snagging a handful every time I was in the boat shop. I carried them down to my office and tossed them in the trash with no compunction.

Hogan smiled, just slightly. "Didn't I see some of these on your desk?"

"Probably." I dumped my purse out on the table. Like most women, I carry far too much junk around.

And, sure enough, in the bottom of the purse there were several ugly chartreuse pencils.

I explained that I'd started a campaign to destroy them. "But some of them do wind up on my desk. Where was that one?"

Hogan and Lieutenant Underwood exchanged looks. Hogan gave a deep sigh.

"When we moved Mrs. Montgomery's body all these things were under it."

"Oh no! That's awesome! I mean awful!" I stopped and took a deep breath. "I'm shocked and horrific. I mean, horrified! And I have no idea how the pencil and the résumé could have gotten there."

"Did you give anyone a pencil?"

"Not that I recall. I suppose I might have dropped one. Or someone might actually have taken one from Joe's shop. He keeps them out in a mug on his desk, but none of those ever seem to go away."

Then I pointed to the letter they had shown me earlier. "What about that?"

"We'll look into it," Hogan said. "You can go on home now, Lee."

I scooped my belongings back into my purse and left. As I went out the door of the little meeting room, Butch got up from a table just outside it. Neither of us spoke, but somehow there was some significant eye contact between us.

Butch went inside the room I'd just left. At that point I realized my car keys had disappeared into the mess in the bottom of my purse. I needed to find them before I left the library so I wouldn't be scrambling around for them in the dark.

I sat down in the chair Butch had been sitting in. It was warm—warm because he had been sitting in it.

Somehow that seemed to be a titillating thought.

I could feel my face flush. It was a stupid thought, I told myself. I ducked my head, hoping the cop guarding the front door wouldn't look at me. I felt as if guilt must be written all over my face. Wasn't lust one of the seven deadly sins?

I dug around inside my purse, but I didn't find the keys. I used the table to dump out the stuff in my purse again, then repacked it, taking time for a little organization. It took me only about a minute. But still I didn't find the keys. They simply were not there.

I made a growling noise and went through everything one more time. Still no keys.

I tried to recall the last time I had had them. I had looked at them when I left Herrera's but decided not to move my car. I'd searched my purse while I was talking to Hogan. Could I have left them in the meeting room?

I hesitated to interrupt Hogan and Lieutenant Underwood. Maybe Butch would come out.

The door to the meeting room was closed, but I heard voices rumble.

I decided that I would have to interrupt. I couldn't simply sit there until Hogan and Lieutenant Underwood stopped questioning Butch.

I went to the door and knocked. Hogan immediately opened the door a crack. He frowned at me, and I suppose he said something. But what I heard was Butch's voice. He wasn't quite yelling.

"I've never heard of Henry C. Dunlap!"

Then Butch went on, his voice just slightly lower. "Lee Woodyard's résumé was on my desk. The vice mayor sent it over for my information. I have no idea how on earth it got into the basement. But I've never seen that letter before."

He sounded adamant. It was a firm denial.

I realized I was staring at him when Hogan touched my arm. "Lee? What do you need?"

"My key card. I mean, my car keys! I must have dropped them in here when I took everything out of my purse."

"I'll look for them," Hogan said. He turned around and looked through the things on the table—papers, evidence sacks, notebooks, and other items. Then he looked in the seats of the chairs nearest the door.

While he did this Lieutenant Underwood was gathering up the papers on the desk—my résumé and the letter, each in a plastic envelope—and putting them into a large plastic bin. And all the time he and Butch were staring at each other like hungry dogs with only one bone between them.

Underwood finally leaned over and looked at Hogan, who by now was looking under the table.

"Chief, what are you doing?"

"Lee's lost her car keys. They could be in here."

Underwood glared at me. He lowered his head below the edge of the table. I came in, got on my knees, and joined the search. "They must have fallen out of my purse when I looked for the pencils."

I tried to sound contrite, but this didn't mollify Underwood. A moment later Butch had joined the search. The four of us were now crawling around on the floor. We weren't dignified, but I finally spotted the keys behind the leg of a chair. Then I bumped my head trying to grab them. It turned into a farce, but I managed to snag the keys and get myself on two feet. Everyone else stood up, and I left.

As the door closed I heard Butch's voice. "Is there anything else, Lieutenant?" He was still sounding authoritative, more authoritative than the cops were. Both

Hogan and Underwood know how to throw their weight around, but neither was choosing to do it right at that moment.

I clutched the keys and turned toward the street door. As I exited I remembered sitting down in the chair Butch had just vacated. The chair with the warm seat.

Lee, I lectured myself, you're a married woman. A happily married woman. What are you doing lusting after a strange man?

I marched up the street to Herrera's parking lot and unlocked the door of my van with a vicious push of the electronic button, telling myself I was a wicked woman.

But by the time I had driven halfway home the lecture had changed. It's normal to notice the opposite sex, I told myself. And you're a normal woman. There's nothing wrong with—well, admiring someone. Nothing wrong unless you act on those feelings.

And I didn't plan to do that. I had wasted five years of my life on one disastrous marriage, though infidelity was the one problem it hadn't had. Now I wanted to be married—happily married—to Joe for the rest of my life. I wasn't going to start ogling sexy guys.

But I couldn't help noticing that they *were* sexy guys. After all, if I caught Joe looking at a pretty girl, I always told him it was okay because I didn't want him to lose interest. That made him laugh. And so far he definitely hadn't lost interest in me. I thought about Joe. He was much better-looking than Butch. And he was as sexy. Forget Butch. I'd go for the guy I already had. Anytime. Like tonight.

But first we had to get Tim handed over to the care of his nephew. And that reminded me that Joe had had a miserable evening. He'd been hauled out by an intoxicated neighbor and asked for transportation so that neighbor, Tim, could see about a family bereavement. He'd helped Tim call his closest relative. He'd worked on sobering Tim up, including taking him out to dinner. He'd picked up the tab—or at least I'd put the dinner on a credit card that was paid by shared family funds. Then he'd had to take Tim home and wait until Hart, Tim's nephew, showed up. If there was any time before Hart arrived, Joe had probably had to spend it talking Tim out of having a few more drinks. Plus I'd called and said I had to go back to talk further to the investigators, so I had been no help at all.

All in all, Joe had had a lousy evening. I needed to tell him I understood this and appreciated all he'd done to help Tim—and me.

I decided the direct approach would be best. I'd just tell Joe how much I appreciated him and that I understood that he'd made an extra effort to be Mr. Nice Guy in a very difficult situation.

Thinking about how wonderful Joe had been actually did make me feel romantic, and this time the focus of my feelings was the right person. I made up a little speech. "Darling, you're the greatest guy in the world. The way you helped Tim was—well, super." That was the beginning.

My plan did not work out.

At least Joe was home when I got there, so I concluded that Hart had showed up to assume responsibility for his uncle.

In fact, Joe had been home long enough to get in the shower. I stood outside the bathroom door and considered getting into it with him. On some occasions, this would have been a good idea, but somehow it didn't seem like a good one that evening. Especially when I tried the door and found it locked.

Hmmm. Unusual.

Then the phone rang. I was surprised, because it was nearly ten o'clock. The caller ID came up with Aunt Nettie's number. I can't ignore Aunt Nettie. So I answered the phone in the kitchen.

"Lee? What's going on down at the library?"

Apparently Hogan had been too busy to call home and give her a report. So I had to do it. And, of course, she had to discuss it.

I paced around the downstairs, phone to ear, while she went over all the disasters that had struck the Hart family in the past few years. When I heard the shower stop, then heard the bathroom door open, I paced even harder.

Finally I said, "Aunt Nettie, I've got to talk to Joe. We'll have to finish this up tomorrow."

I put the phone back where it belonged, then dashed into the bedroom. There was one dim light on my side of the king-sized bed. The room looked romantic.

Except that Joe was already snoring.

I said his name quietly. "Joe."

All the reply I got was, "Hmm?"

I kissed his forehead.

His eyelashes didn't even flicker. "Good night, Lee."

At least he knew who I was. I considered slipping into something sexy and snuggling in beside him. But he had turned with his back to my side of the bed. He gave another snore. He didn't look or sound as if he would respond positively to romantic overtures.

There was always morning. I'd get up early and maybe he'd like a snuggle when he woke up. Then I'd fix pancakes with Michigan maple syrup. That was Joe's favorite breakfast. Even if we didn't have time for early-morning romance, at least I'd get the day off to a good start.

I set my alarm half an hour early and got into bed,

pushing any thought of Butch Cassidy out of my mind. That's hard to do, after all. If you have to keep reminding yourself not to think about a certain topic, it keeps that topic in the forefront of your mind. I checked the alarm four times, afraid I hadn't set it early, but I finally got to sleep.

But by the time my alarm went off the next morning, Joe was up and dressed. The dim light on his side of the bed was on, and he was tying a legal-looking tie around his neck.

I looked at the time, sure I'd overslept. But I hadn't. I had set my alarm half an hour early; Joe apparently had roused himself a half hour before that. I sat up in bed, feeling extremely frowzy, and looked at the time. "How come you're up?"

"I've got a meeting that's going to take some extra time, so I need to get in early."

"Oh. I was going to make pancakes."

"Pancakes are mighty tempting, but I'd better run. I'll grab an Egg McMuffin when I get to Holland."

"Well, darn!"

Joe gave me a quick kiss. He looked serious. "I'll see you tonight."

And he was gone. I was still debating between going back to sleep or getting up early when the lights of his truck went by the window. I lay back down. And darned if Butch Cassidy didn't pop right into my stupid imagination.

I groaned and pulled the pillow over my head.

That morning just didn't want to go right. I fell asleep again and then overslept. I not only didn't get pancakes, but I also didn't even get coffee until I got to TenHuis Chocolade, and I got there twenty minutes late.

Next, Aunt Nettie had to hear all about the events of

the previous evening—again. Her chief assistant, Dolly Jolly, called in sick. An expected delivery of chocolate failed to show, so I had to phone our chocolate supplier and complain. Then the UPS man came to pick up the day's shipments—an hour before they were ready. His usually jovial smile paled when he was told he'd have to come back later.

It was eleven o'clock before something nice happened, and even that happened in the form of a disaster. A Holland florist's shop called, needing an emergency supply of autumn leaves.

Aunt Nettie makes beautiful molded chocolates, different ones for every season of the year. This fall she had produced lovely maple and oak leaves in one-inch, two-inch, and four-inch sizes. They came in white, milk, and dark chocolate and could be purchased wrapped in foil in autumn colors. Arranged in groups they made perfect table decorations or favors for any fall event.

In fact, they were so perfect that the Holland shop had been completely sold out when one of their best customers decided to use the leaves for a big luncheon. Help! They needed more. Two hundred more. Right that moment.

At first I was annoyed and considered a few sharp words about planning ahead, but it's never smart to offer sharp words to a customer. Plus, this gave me an excuse to go to Holland at lunchtime.

I might be able to surprise Joe and take him to lunch.

I checked our stock and cheerfully told the florist I'd personally deliver more leaves. I basked in their gratitude, then loaded the van. I called Joe's cell phone, but it was off. I left a message saying I'd call again or he could return my call, though I didn't say why I was trying to reach him.

The drive to Holland takes a bit over thirty minutes, and Joe hadn't called back by the time I arrived at the florist's shop. I carried the chocolate in, received the owner's enthusiastic thanks, and called Joe again. Still no answer.

I was feeling a bit let down, but I decided to go by his office. It was only twelve o'clock, and Joe usually went to lunch a bit later than that.

His office is in the downtown area, not too far from the courthouse, so parking in the area is at a premium. I found a spot about a half block away, took it, and got out of the van. And miracle of miracles—Joe walked out the door of his office before I stepped onto the curb.

I raised my hand and waved. But I hadn't had a chance to call out Joe's name when a small, slender woman ran across the sidewalk to meet him.

"Joe!" I could hear her enthusiastic greeting. "I'm so glad to see you."

She threw her arms around him and planted a big kiss on his mouth.

And Joe kissed her back.

Chapter 6

After the kiss, Joe smiled broadly. He didn't look at all surprised to see her. The two of them stood together on the sidewalk, practically nose to nose, looking into each other's eyes.

I jumped back in my van so fast I don't think I even opened the door. I kept looking toward Joe and the woman, making sure they hadn't seen me.

The woman was Meg Corbett, the one woman in the world that I feared. Joe's high school girlfriend. Maybe that's all I need to say.

I feared Meg because I thought she might be the one woman in the world that Joe found more attractive than he finds me. She and her husband, Trey Corbett, lived in Warner Pier quite a while. Meg left, more or less under cover of darkness, and maybe it's best not to mention just what happened to Trey. I assumed they were now divorced. I had believed Meg left the state. I had hoped she left the country. At any rate, I didn't want her to pop up in my life again. Or in Joe's.

Not that I had ever had any particular reason to think Joe was still interested in her. Not until I'd seen them greeting each other on the sidewalk in downtown Holland. But a guy never gets over his first . . . well, let's call it his first fling. Maybe he shouldn't get over it.

When I added Meg's personal history to Joe's particular kind of conscience—overactive and idealistic— well, Meg could be the biggest threat my life ever faced. All a girl has to say to Joe is "Help," and he's putty in her hands. And Meg knew it.

I'd already noticed the way Joe reacted if Meg's name came into the conversation. His tone always became contemptuous. Other girls he'd dated brought an amused response, but two of them—Meg, and Joe's first wife, Clementine Ripley—got contempt. I was afraid this meant that they were the two who had really gotten under his skin. They scared me. But Clementine was dead. She wasn't going to appear on Eighth Street in downtown Holland.

Meg was there in the predatory flesh.

So why didn't I confront them? Why did I jump back in my van before either she or Joe could see me?

I guess the smart thing to do would have been to go on walking down the street innocently, to wander up to Joe and Meg and say, "Hi! I didn't know you were back, Meg. I was hoping to go to lunch with Joe. Maybe you can come with us." Or something like that.

I'm brassy, but not quite that brassy. I wasn't ready to confront Meg, not a Meg with a proprietary hand on Joe's arm, looking deeply into his eyes. I couldn't do it. Not with my heart sinking down around my knees. I'd have to steel myself.

Anyway, Joe and Meg walked on up the block— thank goodness they didn't come toward me—arm in arm. As soon as they had disappeared, I started back to Warner Pier. I didn't stop on the way. I had lost all interest in lunch, but as soon as I got to my desk I ate both of my daily pieces of TenHuis chocolate.

TenHuis allows each employee to have two of our luscious bonbons and truffles every day. I never forget. That day I ate an Amaretto truffle ("milk chocolate filling flavored with almond liqueur, in a milk chocolate shell, and embellished with chopped almonds"). Then I scarfed down a caramel truffle ("gooey soft caramel filling in a dark chocolate shell, trimmed with a milk chocolate swirl").

Both were darn good and ultra sweet. I felt a little better after I had eaten them.

I went into the ladies' room, the only place at Ten-Huis Chocolade that has a mirror, and I looked at myself. I looked okay. I didn't think anybody, even Aunt Nettie, would be able to see the turmoil inside. That was good. I didn't want to display my troubles. Certainly not my troubles with Joe.

If I did have troubles with Joe. I reminded myself that I didn't know that. Meg could simply be consulting Joe professionally. She might have just dropped by to catch up on old high school friends. She could be looking for a job and hoping that Joe could refer her to someone who was hiring.

But I didn't believe any of those things. I'd seen the way she was looking at Joe, and I'd seen the way he was looking back. I'd seen the way she grabbed him and the kiss she gave him. The looks they'd been exchanging hadn't been those of a lawyer and a casual client, or of two old chums.

I brushed my hair into a sort of queue, à la George Washington, and fastened it with a barrette. I freshened my makeup. And I went back to work, feeling brave. By quitting time, I told myself, I would have figured out how to deal with this problem.

In the meantime, I had a surprise visit. A good-looking guy with prematurely gray hair came in the front door of the shop. It was Hart VanHorn, the nephew of the library board member who had apparently been murdered.

I left my desk and went out into the shop to greet him. I had met Hart a few months after I moved to Michigan. He'd even asked me out—once—and I had agreed to go. But life intervened before Hart and I kept that date, and by the time things settled down, we'd both realized that we could be friends, but romance wasn't in the picture.

In a way, I owed my marriage to Hart. At the time Hart asked me out, Joe had been showing interest in me, but he kept shying away from asking me out. After Hart made his move, Joe suddenly got a lot bolder. He managed to store some of the baggage from his first marriage high in the attic. He made me feel valued and pursued. And all because Hart's interest made Joe realize I wasn't Miss Plain Jane sitting home, waiting for his call. Apparently he also realized that he didn't want to lose me.

I shook Hart's hand and murmured the conventional words. "I'm so sorry, Hart."

"I wanted to thank you for the things you did last night. Taking care of Tim."

"Joe handled that. I'll tell him what you said."

"And I appreciate your staying with Abby until the authorities came."

"I don't deserve thanks for that." I leaned closer and whispered, "I did it to keep Miss Vanderklomp from doing it, and it was sheer obnoxiousness on my part."

Hart smiled. "I understand. I've had my run-ins

with Miss Vanderklomp. Anybody who can stand up to her has my respect."

"Come on in my office. Could I offer you a cup of coffee?"

"That sounds great."

I beckoned to one of the ladies who make the chocolates. "Would you tell Aunt Nettie that Hart VanHorn is here? She'll want to speak to him. And I know it's not your job, but could you bring us some coffee?"

Each request drew a "ya, shure," which is the West Michigan way of saying "I'd be glad to."

Hart was already seated in my office when I went back to my desk. "How's Tim today?"

"Really down, of course. It's hard to lose your final sibling. Even one who never had much to say. But what I can't grasp is that Hogan Jones is hinting that someone might have deliberately killed Abby! That's just impossible!"

"They won't say anything until after the autopsy."

"Abby was a truly inoffensive person. She never flashed her opinions around. Or she didn't in front of me." Hart grimaced. "The effect of growing up with my mother as an older sister, I guess. Mother was Miss Opinionated from childhood on."

I nodded. Silence was best on the subject of Hart's mother. "Everyone on the library board reacted the way you are," I said. "They said Mrs. Montgomery was easygoing. But they also said that if she felt strongly about something, she stood up for it."

"That's true. I remember— Well, when my grandmother died, Aunt Abby and my mother both laid claim to a small desk. For all her quiet nature, Aunt Abby won. That desk is in her house today."

I chuckled. And in a moment Hart continued. "Now

I wish I'd known her better. But she lived in California until she retired."

"Oh, she had a career?"

"Yes. Aunt Abby had a business degree and worked for an accounting firm. After Uncle Bill died she sold up in California and came back here. They never had kids. I don't even know if she had a will."

"Will she have provided for Tim?"

"That's possible, but Tim's trust keeps him going. She might have left her assets to the dog and cat home. Or I might be the heir."

"Probably the executor, too." I decided it was time to change the subject. "Has Tim figured out what Mrs. Montgomery was worried about?"

"What do you mean?"

"When he and Joe got to the library last night, the first thing Tim said to me was 'Now I'll never know what Abby was worried about.' Didn't he mention it to you?"

"No. That's peculiar."

"I wonder if he said anything about it to Hogan."

"Maybe not. I'll ask him. Or, better still, I'll ask Hogan."

The coffee arrived right at that moment, carried by Aunt Nettie. She sat down with us, made sympathetic noises, and offered Hart chocolates. After a few minutes Hart said he needed to go, so she tried to press a box of chocolates on him.

Hart assured her that sweets weren't needed. "Tim's house is already loaded with food from the neighbors," he said. "Mother's house is closed up, but luckily the electricity is still connected, so we've plugged in the fridge. We'll have to clean out the one at Abby's and use that, too."

"I'm a neighbor, too," I said. "If you need someone to help sort things out, give me a holler."

"Aunt Abby had a cleaning woman, so I'll get her to come. But I'll call on you if I need to."

Hart went away in a few minutes, looking solemn, and I carried the coffee cups to the kitchen. I could still feel the big lump I'd had in my chest since I saw Joe with Meg Corbett, but it didn't feel quite so big. After all, the Harts and the VanHorns were important people, and they had troubles. Why would I think I would escape?

But in a way I could have coped with a murder more easily than with the idea of Joe and Meg meeting surreptitiously. I toyed with the idea of confiding in Aunt Nettie. I knew she'd reassure me, tell me there was an innocent explanation. Like Joe and Meg were planning a class reunion.

I'd never believe that. I decided not to consult Aunt Nettie.

I got back to my desk just as the phone rang. It was Hogan. "Hey, Lee, can you come over to the station for a minute?"

"Do I need to sign a statement?"

"We've got a couple more questions."

Click. I growled. Now what? As if I weren't already upset, between having to sit with a dead body and discovering my husband prancing down the main street of Holland with an old girlfriend . . . Now I had to answer more questions.

I was so annoyed that I spoke aloud. "Rats! I've told you all every single thing I know!"

I stomped my feet with every step I took toward the police station, and I had to try hard to keep from swinging the door to the police station open and slamming it against the wall.

And when I got inside, Hogan was closed up in his office with somebody, so I had to sit and wait. That didn't make me any happier, but it gave me a chance to catch my breath and think quiet thoughts and remind myself that I'd be foolish to pitch a fit at Hogan. First, he was my uncle—sort of—and I didn't want a quarrel in the family. Second, Hogan was Authority—the police chief of the town where I lived. Third, I liked him. But he sure was hitting me at a time when I didn't want to talk about his concerns. I wanted to worry about mine.

In a few minutes the door opened, and Butch Cassidy came out. He turned back to speak to Hogan. "Frankly, Chief Jones, I hope this is the last time we talk for a while."

"I'd like nothing better," Hogan said. He gestured toward me. "Lee, come on in."

Butch and I had to pass by each other as I went in and he went out. Our eyes met. Yes, I felt a certain spark. Darn it.

Lieutenant Underwood wasn't in the office. This pleased me. I was happier facing Hogan alone, without that particular state police detective.

Hogan opened the conversation. "Lee, do you remember my showing you a letter last night?"

"Sure. At least, I saw an envelope addressed to Henry Somebody. In a plastic envelope."

"You didn't touch it?"

"Of course not!"

"You didn't see anybody else touch it?"

"No. Why? What happened to it?"

"We're not sure. It's gone."

"That's funny. Could it have dropped in the street?"

"No, Lee. We've looked. It wasn't dropped in the street. It's not under the rug. It's not behind a bookcase. And the dog didn't eat it."

I looked at Hogan narrowly. "Oh," I said. "Sarcasm."

Hogan glared. "The last time it was seen, you and this Cassidy guy were there."

"I didn't take it."

"That's what he says, too."

That's when I lost my temper. "As my grandmother used to say, Hogan, 'You're getting my dandruff up.' I did not mess with your evidence. I know nothing about any Henry Whoever. I never saw that envelope except when you showed it to me. I do not know where it disappeared to. And as far as I know, the dog did eat it!"

I took a deep breath, glared, and continued talking. "I wouldn't touch your lousy evidence, and you know it!"

Hogan then lost his temper. "Lee, I know you and Nettie are closer than mother and daughter. And I don't want to get into it with you, because it could really give me trouble at home. But I can't just let this slide! That letter was there, and now it's not. Something happened to it. Underwood and I have looked everywhere. The state police tech looked everywhere. It's gone! And I can't just say, 'Oh, Lee Woodyard wouldn't take it. She's my wife's niece.' You can't have a special dispensation."

"I'm not asking for one! You can investigate all you want! Do you want to search me? My car? My house? Go for it! But I did not take that envelope. And I don't appreciate your not taking my word for it."

I stood up. "And now I'm leaving. Unless I need to get a lawyer."

"Go! Go! We're obviously not getting anywhere. But unless that envelope turns up, I'll have to ask you about it again."

I walked out. Out of Hogan's office and out of the police station. I was so angry with Hogan that I think I had tears in my eyes.

And the reason I was so angry with Hogan was that

I was angry with Joe over his meeting with Meg. Yes, it was illogical. One situation had nothing to do with the other. But I couldn't yell at Joe, so I yelled at Hogan. It was stupid, but that's the way I felt.

I considered going home, where I could rant, rave, and cry in private. I wanted to bang my head against one of the show windows of the stores I was walking past. I wanted to bang Joe's head against one of those show windows. I was worried, and I didn't have the slightest idea how to deal with my problem.

But I didn't go home. I went to TenHuis Chocolade, and the aroma of chocolate swept over me as I went in the door. Instead of being tempting and soothing, as it usually is, it made me feel nauseated.

I must be sick. I decided I would go home after all. I'd just take the rest of the day off. I'd go home and feel sorry for myself.

I started into the workroom, so I could tell Aunt Nettie I was leaving.

But the counter girl caught me. "Lee," she said, "you have a visitor."

I must have looked dismayed. I carefully turned my back on the glass cubicle that held my desk. "Who is it?" I said.

The girl leaned close. "It's that old teacher," she said. "Miss Vanderklomp."

Chapter 7

My heart sank. I didn't want to see anybody at all, and I definitely didn't want to see Miss Vander-klomp.

But it was too late. I heard her voice. "Mrs. Wood-yard! Mrs. Woodyard!"

I turned toward her. I couldn't force a smile, but I tried to look pleasant. "Hello, Miss Vanderklomp." I walked into the office, dragging my feet as if I were going to the guillotine, and sat down behind my desk. "How can I help you?"

Miss Vanderklomp adjusted her bra straps and picked up her water holder, the one that supposedly held Pepsi. "I need some information," she said, "and it occurred to me that you might be able to help me."

"If I can. What did you need to know?"

"I gather that the law enforcement officials are likely to search the basement of the library."

"I imagine they've already done that."

Miss Vanderklomp looked startled. "What? There

were no official cars there this morning. Would they have searched during the night?"

Belatedly I remembered that no official announcement had been made on the cause of Abigail Montgomery's death. Miss Vanderklomp probably believed that she died in an accident. Besides, she apparently knew nothing about police procedure, so she wouldn't understand the significance of searching the basement.

I also remembered that Hogan had asked me not to reveal what he believed was the real cause of death.

"Well, you see . . ." I stuttered around. "Hogan called in the state police's lab men just to look the situation over. They were there last night. So while the scene was fresh, I imagine they went over it pretty thoroughly."

Miss Vanderklomp looked affronted. "I really cannot imagine that valuable police skills and time were spent on the scene of an accidental death."

"Yes, it's hard to understand."

"That basement is extensive. My grandfather used to store produce in it." Miss Vanderklomp chuckled. "I hardly think they would search the entire room."

"I wouldn't want to guess at how extensive their search was. I know they were working there last night for several hours."

"Hmmm. The basement door is now marked as off-limits, sealed with that yellow tape. How soon do you think they will permit access to library board members and volunteers?"

"I have no idea. Miss Vanderklomp, why are you asking me all these questions? You need to be asking Chief Jones directly."

Miss Vanderklomp gave a nervous laugh. "I didn't want to bother him."

So you bother me instead? I resisted the temptation to throw something at her.

"The chief is the only one who knows what's going on in the investigation into Mrs. Montgomery's death. If you want an authoritative answer, you'll have to ask him."

"Why do they need some detailed investigation? It was just an accidental death!"

"The cause of death won't be official until the medical examiner rules on it. The medical examiner must have come last night, but apparently there won't be an official ruling until they've completed an autopsy."

That was as close as I could come to telling her Abigail Montgomery had been murdered. But she didn't seem to catch on. She looked horrified, true, but it apparently wasn't the idea of murder that caused her reaction.

"An autopsy?"

"Perhaps not a complete autopsy, but a pathologist will be determining the cause of death."

"I'm shocked! I can't believe that a man of Hart Van-Horn's influence will permit that."

"Hart's an attorney. He knows that they have to follow the law."

"But you're making it sound as if Abigail's death involved some sort of . . ." Miss Vanderklomp paused and lowered her voice. "Some sort of foul play."

"Until the medical examiner rules on a cause of death and the state police report on their preliminary findings, that remains a possibility."

"But it's ridiculous!" She lowered her voice some more. Apparently I was to receive an important confidence. "I have some important personal items stored in that basement. I need to access them."

"You can talk to Chief Jones. He might let you in."

"Would he want to accompany me?"

"I don't know."

Miss Vanderklomp bit her lip. "I need to visit the basement privately."

"Miss Vanderklomp, I really have nothing to do with all this. I'm just describing what I've learned by watching other investigations and by talking to Chief Jones in an informal way. You need to take this up with him directly."

"Oh no!" She leaped to her feet. "No, that would never do."

She left the office without another comment. I belatedly realized that I hadn't even offered her chocolate.

I also realized—as my temper cooled—that the whole episode cast an odd light on Miss Vanderklomp. She had acted unsure of herself. She had been hesitant to call Hogan and demand what she wanted. She didn't seem to want to talk to him, much less request any favors.

Why? Why was the dominant and domineering Miss Ann Vanderklomp—fabled for her imitation of a human bulldozer—hesitant to call her city's police chief and ask a favor? Normally I'd expect her to march into the police station and make demands.

A thought came to me, but I brushed it away. It was impossible. Miss Vanderklomp acted as if she were afraid.

I assured myself that couldn't be true. It would be completely out of character. But what else could explain her attitude? Miss Vanderklomp had definitely wanted into that basement before the police got there. The news that they'd probably already searched it had been unwelcome. It hadn't exactly sent her into a panic, but she sure hadn't liked it.

Maybe I should have told her that she had nothing to worry about. Butch and I were the obvious suspects.

I got to my feet, still determined to go home and eat worms. What a lousy day this had been. And what could I do about it? I couldn't think of anything.

I told Aunt Nettie I was leaving, instructed the counter girl to catch the telephone, and headed out. I don't think I even knew where I was going. The rednecks who hang out in my dad's garage back in Texas would have said I was lower than a snake's belly.

I simply had to do something to cheer up.

So I went to the beach.

Our house is on Lakeshore Drive. Every town around Lake Michigan has a Lakeshore Drive or a Lake Shore Drive. Our house is on the inland, or low-rent side. Property with lake views is a lot more valuable, but our side is fine. We can walk to a public-access area of the beach in ten minutes, and we don't have to pay the taxes the people with a view of the water do.

So I drove to Beech Tree Public Access Area, the beach near our house. The day was sunny, the autumn light was beautiful, the foliage was beginning to turn gorgeous, and that afternoon the temperature was in the mid-sixties. I kicked off my shoes, rolled up my jeans, went down the stairs to the beach, and walked in the sand.

My situation seemed a little better already. Okay, I asked myself, what's the worst thing that can happen?

Well, Joe could leave me for Meg. The thought made me feel as if I'd been kicked in the middle.

But awful as that would be, I knew I'd go on living. I wouldn't live very happily, but I'd still breathe and sleep and eat and survive, just as I would if someone close to me died.

What could I do about that situation? First, I wasn't remotely sure that was a threat. Second, if it was a threat, I didn't exactly understand what Meg's attraction was, so I wasn't sure how to counter it. And if Joe was involved with Meg, did I even want him back? Would our relationship be destroyed in any case?

That situation was the worst thing I had to face, and all I had was a bunch of questions and no answers. I decided to worry about something else.

The other problem of the day was how the detectives investigating Abigail Montgomery's death could think I had interfered with their evidence.

I considered the missing evidence, the letter that had disappeared. Was I really suspected of taking it? Nah, I told myself. That wasn't too likely. Hogan knows—in his heart of hearts—that I wouldn't do that. They might ask me a bunch of questions, but I was telling the truth. I hadn't taken the mysterious letter addressed to Henry C. Whoever.

Did the missing letter make me a suspect in her death?

It was hard to believe that I'd be a suspect in Abigail's death at all, since I had never met the woman while she was alive. But I knew from my association with Hogan that one of the main factors in a murder investigation was opportunity. MOM, he said. Means, opportunity, and motive.

Well, the means of Abigail's death—the rod from the magazine rack—was handy for anybody who went into the basement and wanted to use it. And I certainly had the opportunity. I could easily have wandered down there before the library board meeting began.

Anybody who had been in the library building before the board meeting could have gone into the basement, met Abigail, quarreled with her, and hit her in the head with a handy wooden rod.

But I had no motive at all.

I walked along, sticking to the sandy areas of the beach and avoiding the rocky areas. Those rocks might have been smoothed by the ancient glaciers, but they were mighty hard on bare feet. I kept my head down, looking at where I was stepping.

Which will have to be my excuse for almost falling over someone I knew.

I had become vaguely aware that someone was sitting on a driftwood log ahead of me, but I had my head ducked, so I hadn't taken in any details.

I was within fifteen feet of the person when I heard a deep voice. "Hello, Mrs. Woodyard. Lee."

I looked up and saw Butch Cassidy.

"Oh! I didn't see you. I mean, I didn't see who was there. What a coherence! I mean, what a coincidence."

"I guess we both felt the need for a little fresh air after our sessions with the cops."

"I often come here. It's close to our house." I walked a step closer. "Where are you living?"

"For the moment I'm in a place owned by Rhonda Ringer-Riley. She calls it a summer rental. I think this means I need to get out before the first hard freeze."

I smiled, but I was afraid that he was right. The Ringer-Riley place—a house with several small cottages Rhonda rented to tourists—was a mile south of us on Lake Shore Drive.

"Do you have heat?"

"Yes, there's an electric heater. So far the house has been very comfortable. And I have lake access. I walked up the shore. I hope I'm not trespassing."

"I think you're legal. As I understand it, the water

and the area right along it are public, so anybody can walk up and down. You might have trouble if you go up toward one of the houses along the bluff."

I turned to see exactly where we were and saw the corner of a large brick house about thirty feet above us. "Oh, golly! We're right beside Abigail Montgomery's house. Talk about fate! She's haunting us."

Butch groaned, put his elbows on his knees, and dropped his head to his hands. "What a mess!"

Butch was attractive even when he was discouraged. I gave a silly giggle. "Don't despair! If you're worried about that letter—well, I imagine that Lieutenant Underwood dropped it on the way to the car. Eventually they'll figure out that it had nothing to do with either of us."

Butch looked up. "Oh, they'll figure it out sooner, rather than later. I've decided I have to go explain."

"Explain?"

"Yes. When everybody dropped to their knees to look for your keys . . . Well, the letter was the second thing in the bin of plastic envelopes. I just slid it inside my jacket and walked off with it. I'm the one who took the mysterious letter."

Chapter 8

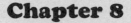

I was so surprised that I nearly collapsed in the sand.
Actually, I did collapse as far as dropping my fanny
onto the tree trunk. I perched on the opposite end from
where Butch was sitting, and I stared at him.

Finally I spoke. "You took it! Why?"

Butch gave me an annoyed look.

"Oh! Right," I said. "You didn't want the cops to
look at it."

And the reason he didn't want the cops to see it was
obviously none of my business.

"There's nothing in it that's incriminating," Butch said.
"I haven't murdered anybody—not Abigail Montgomery
or anybody else. I haven't blackmailed, stolen, perjured,
defrauded, or done anything else illegal. I just didn't want
them to see that letter."

"So you took it."

"Yes, and now I see that taking it was incredibly stupid. I took it because I knew it had nothing to do with
Mrs. Montgomery's death, and I thought it might mis-

lead the detectives. Now I see that by making it disappear, I gave it an artificial importance."

"The effect turned out to be the opposite of what you wanted."

"Exactly. And I inadvertently involved you. But don't worry. I'll go back and tell Chief Jones what I did. At least that will get you off the hook."

I stared at the lake. Butch had acted stupidly, but who among us hasn't? I've certainly done things impulsively, then regretted them.

Butch spoke again. "I'm really sorry, because I think the letter will focus attention on something extraneous, a situation that can't possibly have any relation to the death of Abigail Montgomery."

"Are you sure of that?"

"As sure as I can be. The letter was on my desk. I don't know how it got to the basement."

"You didn't have it in your pocket when we went downstairs?"

"No. And even if it had been there, I did not touch Mrs. Montgomery's body. I don't see how the letter could have simply fallen where the police found it. Someone had to bring it downstairs."

"Mrs. Montgomery?"

"Either her or her attacker. One of them must have been holding it when she was attacked. If she was attacked. But however it got there, I need to return it to the investigators."

An idea was beginning to glimmer on the periphery of my brain. I stared over the water and mulled like mad.

Butch sighed deeply and stood up. "I guess I'd better just go face the music."

"Wait a minute! Let me think."

"I've got to return it. That's the only answer."

"Maybe not. Have you opened the evidence envelope?"

"No."

"Then give it to me, and I'll return it."

"Why?"

"I'll tell 'em I found it in my purse."

"What!"

"And I'll say I have no idea how it got there."

"But it's not fair for you to get involved."

"It won't involve me. It will simply be some accident that happened when we were all looking for the keys. I can say I have no recollection of picking it up. But there it was, way in the bottom of my purse."

"Do you think that will work?"

"Do you have a different plan? One that won't mislead Hogan and the state detectives?"

"I'll feel guilty if you get in trouble."

"Don't be silly! I'm the one person in all this that is, well, above suspicion. They'll just think I'm my usual flaky self. I have no motive for either killing Abigail Montgomery or for hiding whoever did kill her."

Butch and I looked at each other. And darn it! I did have a motive. I hadn't been so attracted to a man in . . . well, maybe never. I wanted to grab him and throw him down on the sand. And, by golly, the look he was giving me told me he felt the same way.

We sat there for a long minute, gazing into each other's eyes.

I blinked first. "Now," I said, "how do I get hold of the letter?"

"It happens that I have it on me." Butch reached under his sweatshirt and pulled out the plastic container that held the envelope. "I was afraid to leave it lying around."

"Wipe it off," I said. "Here. I'll use my scarf. Then on the remote chance that they find fibers on the envelope, they'll be from something that could have been in my purse."

I spread the scarf on the sand, then laid the plastic on it and rubbed both sides with the other end of the scarf. I picked up the envelope.

"Now it'll have your fingerprints on it!"

"That's okay. I had to take it out of my purse, right? It would logically have my fingerprints on it. Of course, it should have several cops' prints on it, too. We'll have to trust to luck on that."

I stood up. "I hope you realize this puts you completely in my power. You'll have to trust me not to betray you."

"I'm already completely in your power." Butch gave me a look that made me hold my breath. What did he mean by that?

Then he grinned. "Board members rule!" he said.

I breathed again. "I'm not a board member yet."

I stuck the plastic envelope and its contents under my own sweatshirt and tucked it into my jeans. It seemed to burn a patch on my stomach. Butch and I gave each other a casual wave and walked away in opposite directions.

I went straight back to the van, got into it, and drove directly to the Warner Pier Police Department. I did this because I had decided to tell one of my favorite people a lie, and I was afraid I'd lose my nerve if I thought about it too long.

I guess I was lucky. Hogan wasn't there. So I wrote a note—"I found this in my purse. I have no idea how it got there."—and left the letter, still in its plastic sleeve, with the receptionist.

Then I went home. My conscience was bothering me

because I was lying, but I decided it would be bothering me even more if I hadn't connived with Butch to return the letter. My feelings for Butch already had my conscience riled up, but I had no intention of acting on them. Or so I told myself.

I decided I needed to occupy my mind. I didn't want to think about that letter in its plastic sleeve. If I got busy, it would help me forget it. I decided I'd actually cook a decent dinner for Joe.

No, this had nothing to do with his meeting with Meg. I wasn't going to do the happy-homemaker act, trying to convince Joe that domesticity was more attractive than the titillation of illicit meetings with former girlfriends. I'd tried the domestic act with a different husband, and I wasn't any good at it. I'm an accountant, not a domestic goddess.

The dinner plan really had very little to do with Joe. On that particular day I was the one who wanted the illusion of a happy home. And to me that meant chicken-fried steak, mashed potatoes, and green beans. Luckily, I had all the ingredients on hand, including minute steaks, cooking oil, and a bit of bacon fat for flavor, plus my Michigan grandmother's big iron skillet. I floured and fried the steak, measured the flour and milk for the cream gravy, simmered the green beans, and peeled the potatoes.

I put the potatoes on to boil when I saw Joe pull into the drive. He came in the back door, pulling off his lawyer tie. "Hi," he said. "I'm feeling a bit guilty."

I felt a bit relieved. Ha, I thought. He's going to tell me about seeing Meg and reassure me that it meant nothing. But I played innocent. "What do you feel guilty about?"

"You called me a couple of times, and I never got a chance to call back."

Oh. He wasn't talking about Meg.

Joe spoke again. "I hope you didn't need anything important."

"I'd have kept calling if I had. I called because I had to make an unexpected trip to Holland late in the morning, so I wondered if you were available for lunch." I stared at the potatoes.

"Oh. Sorry I missed the calls. But I was stuck with a client anyway."

A client? Meg was to be an anonymous client?

Joe went on. "It sure smells good in here. Have I got time to change clothes before dinner?"

I assured Joe the dinner would be another half hour, and he wandered on into the bedroom. I knew he'd come out shortly in jeans and an old M-Go-Blue sweat-shirt.

Once I had the potatoes on and Joe had changed clothes and pulled a beer from the refrigerator, we sat on the screened porch. Evenings would soon be too cool for relaxing outside.

The conversation started routinely. Joe asked if I'd had a rough day.

"I got distracted by the investigation into Abigail Montgomery's death," I said, "and I wound up coming home early. How was your day?"

"Nothing too crazy."

"How was Meg?"

The question slipped right out without my being aware that it was going to. But as soon as I heard it I realized that I had planned to say something about her all the time. I just had to. I'm not sneaky by nature, and I certainly am not going to start being sneaky with Joe. If we can't be honest—all the time—the jig is already up on our marriage.

Joe's face got really blank. I guess lawyers have to

take Deadpan 101 in their final year in law school. He is able to completely lose all expression. He can also hide behind a smile or a frown, but he does that more rarely.

He didn't answer my question about Meg right away, but I didn't repeat it. He put on a grin, sort of like slipping into a jacket, before he finally replied. "I guess you came by the office and saw her."

I nodded.

"Why didn't you stop and join us?"

"I thought about it, but it looked as if the two of you were headed for lunch, and I guess lunch with Meg didn't appeal to me. So? How is she?"

"She's broke, and she's finally getting a divorce."

I nodded. "I figured. Did she make money when she sold the house down here?"

"Nope. It had a big mortgage, so it didn't bring in much, and she let that go to Trey for his legal fees."

"I'm surprised."

"I was surprised, too. She does have a job—hostess at a nice restaurant—but her income definitely qualifies her for our client list."

"That must be a blow to Meg."

"Yep. I think she's looking for a better job." Joe took a drink of his beer. "When she came to the agency, she requested that I work with her."

Joe didn't appear to see that his two sentences might be connected. I decided not to comment on them. "Do you think that's wise? After all, her ex tried to kill you."

"I still don't think Meg knew about that."

I had my doubts about that, and Joe was aware of them. I decided no comment was needed.

"We'll see how it works," Joe said. "Frankly, you don't seem very pleased."

I pondered my answer, and my hesitation probably

confirmed my displeasure at Joe's contact with Meg. As I said, I didn't want to be sneaky. Still, I couldn't bring myself to be completely honest. No, I couldn't bring myself to say, "I'm jealous of Meg. I don't want her in your life, even professionally, because I'm afraid you are still attracted to her. I wish she was in Timbuktu."

So I measured my words carefully and finally spoke. "Joe, I've never made any pretense of liking Meg. Naturally, I wish she hadn't turned up again. But I don't wish her ill. If you can help her get her life back on track, I guess you need to do it."

"I just hope my mom can maintain that calm an attitude if she finds out."

"You have to handle your mom," I said. "I'm not tangling with her."

"I just can't understand why good women want to keep a person like Meg down."

"What do you mean?"

"I'm talking about Mom, I guess. She always disliked Meg, always tried to warn me against her. She said it was because Meg didn't have any family background. As if my mom came from some elite family. My grandfather had a boat shop, and my mom never went to college! Mom judged Meg strictly by her mother. And I admit Meg's mother was a mess."

"You're talking about when you and Meg were in high school."

"Right!"

"Joe, if you had a smart and handsome teenaged son, and you saw him falling for a girl who was born out of wedlock, whose mother seems to have been on welfare, whose family—"

"See? Everybody judges Meg by her family!"

I opened my mouth, ready to reply. There was certainly a lot more to be said on this topic. But would that be smart?

I snapped my jaw shut. "I'll check on the potatoes," I said. "They might be ready to mash."

Chocolate Chat

Manufacturers come up with the darnedest things, and apparently they think consumers will go for anything if they add chocolate to it.

Chocolate mixed with cream cheese is now on the market. In Europe this product is sold as a breakfast item; in America, it's marketed as a snack, to be used with pretzels or fruit.

Or how about chocolate pasta? One chef added cocoa powder to pasta and found he had a hit. It's not sweet. The cocoa powder reportedly gives the noodles or macaroni a slightly bitter flavor. It can be ordered online.

Then there are fake chocolate items. For example, mirrors, cell phone cases, or cosmetics cases made to look like chocolate bars. Evening bags have been made in the shape of candy boxes and may have photos of truffles and bonbons printed on the outside. My favorite: a calculator with keys that look like bits of chocolate. Yes, the "chocolate" keys have numbers and other symbols printed on them. Perfect for counting calories, right?

There are also objects to add to home décor. Coasters shaped like squares of chocolate, throw rugs that look like candy bars, and, yes, bonbon wallpaper.

Chapter 9

When I got to the kitchen, my brain felt as if it were the same consistency as the potatoes I was mashing.

Joe was on the defensive about Meg. There were two obvious reasons. One, he was sexually attracted to her. Two, he felt protective about her because of their youthful relationship.

And maybe both were a factor. But in any case, this could be a crisis for our marriage.

Although Joe had been railing at his mother's attitude toward Meg, I was aware that his anger was also directed toward me. Joe thought I had much the same attitude toward Meg that his mother did. He was trying to avoid an open quarrel with me, but he saw how unhappy I was about Meg's reappearance, and he resented it.

Joe usually handles his life very sensibly, but he'd blown it over the matter of Meg.

Why hadn't he just told me Meg had showed up as a client and he took her to lunch? Why did he get mad when I talked to him about her? I'd tried to be rational and nonaccusatory, but he'd gone into this tirade about his mom being prejudiced against Meg—eighteen years ago.

Was it because he and Meg had begun an affair? The suspicion stabbed me right in the gizzard, but I forced myself to face it.

And I decided it was unlikely. Joe admitted that, as a college jock, he had not been in the habit of going home alone. But he seemed to have lost his taste for casual sex in his mid-twenties, before he married for the first time.

No, what worried me about Meg wasn't that she and Joe might visit the local motel for a quickie. It was that Meg touched Joe on a much deeper level. I was afraid he might fall in love with her.

For that matter, did I have the right to suspect Joe of unfaithfulness when I'd spent much of the previous evening and the current day feeling lustful toward another man?

Well, I hadn't considered doing anything about it. Anything specific. Except tell the law enforcement authorities an out-and-out lie.

Would I have done that if I hadn't been strongly attracted to Butch Cassidy?

Heck, no!

I growled. The whole thing was too big a mess for me to figure out on an empty stomach. I mashed the potatoes hard, then added milk and butter and whipped the dickens out of them. Food. I needed food. Specifically, down-home Texas comfort food.

"Dinner," I said loudly, "is served."

Chicken-fried steak, cream gravy, mashed potatoes, and green beans. Yum. Yum. This might not be as comforting a meal to Joe as it is to me, since he was brought up in Michigan, and that state's semiofficial favorite dish is brats and sauerkraut. But no person with operational taste buds can say chicken-fried steak isn't good. Joe got to the table as soon as I did, and we both chowed down.

This is not a meal I cook often. Too many calories. It's a once-in-a-while treat, unless the diners are spending their days digging ditches. With shovels. But when you need comfort, it's the best.

Worried as I was, I hadn't lost my appetite, and Joe hadn't lost his either. We had both cleaned our plates when headlights flashed on the living room windows.

"Were you expecting anybody?" Joe looked out the window. "Like Hogan?"

My heart sank. I assumed that Hogan had come by to talk to me. He must not be buying my story about finding the missing letter in the bottom of my purse.

I heard a car door slam. Just one door. At least Hogan had come alone. He hadn't dragged Lieutenant Larry Underwood along. I'd have to lie to only one person.

However, that person was a man I loved and respected like a second father.

But I had to do it. I was committed. To Butch.

I took a deep breath and opened the back door. "Hi," I said. "Have you had dinner?"

"Nettie fed me."

"We're ready for dessert, and I was thinking about putting on the coffeepot. Want to join us?"

Hogan sighed as he came in the door. "Coffee sounds pretty good, Lee. If I have a cup, maybe I'll figure out a way to convince Larry Underwood that you don't know anything about our new homicide."

"Well, that ought to be simple, since I really don't know anything about it."

Hogan was in the house before I got a look at Joe's face. He'd completely lost his deadpan expression.

That's when I realized that Joe still thought that Abigail Montgomery died from a fall down the stairs. We hadn't talked about it the previous evening, in front of Tim, and apparently he hadn't heard anything about it that day.

But when Joe spoke, his voice was calm. Maybe even cold. "I can't believe Lee thought you might suspect she was mixed up in a homicide, Hogan. We've been talking for an hour, and she's never mentioned it."

I'd been chided.

Hogan looked from one of us to the other.

I turned away and got the coffeepot. "Joe, if you'd clear the table, it would be a big help," I said.

The three of us talked about the weather or some similar subject until the coffee was made, the dishes from the table were in the sink, and I'd put a dozen TenHuis chocolates on a plate. I sublimated all thoughts of murder and thought about foil-wrapped autumn leaves and Asian spice truffles ("milk chocolate centers flavored with ground ginger and enrobed with milk chocolate"). Of course, the truffles I offered were not decorated the way they should have been, and the designs on the autumn leaves had smudged. Everybody makes a mistake now and then, and chocolate-company employees get to bring home the unsellable stuff for free. I'm definitely too cheap to pay even employee-discount rates just to get out of making dessert.

After we were settled in the living room with our coffee and goodies, I quickly jumped in before Hogan could and asked the first question. "You're now calling Abigail Montgomery's death a homicide. The last time I saw you, it was still a probable homicide. So I gather you have new evidence."

"We got a preliminary report from the medical examiner. The fatal wound definitely did not come from falling down the stairs."

I shuddered. "Is the wooden stick from the newspaper rack the weapon?"

"The tests aren't complete, but that seems likely."

"Did I ruin the fingerprints?"

"Yours were the only ones on it. I think it had been thoroughly wiped before you picked it up."

Joe was looking more and more amazed. "How did I miss all this?"

I tried not to sound sarcastic. "You haven't been around."

Yes, the night before, Joe had gone to bed without speaking to me, and that morning he'd left while I was still in bed. Our predinner conversation had been on another important matter. Communication had been lacking.

"Besides," I said, "Hogan said he didn't want it to be public knowledge." I quickly asked Hogan another question. "Has any particular suspect emerged?"

"It's got to be one of the people who were at the library yesterday evening."

"Nobody could have snuck in the back way?"

"It doesn't seem likely. And the general public wasn't present. The custodian at that church across the alley was working outside, and he didn't see anybody."

"People were lined up to check out books as I came in."

"Yes, and because they checked out books, we knew who they were. Apparently all of them had gone out the front door before Mrs. Montgomery went down to the basement."

"How do you know?"

"Mrs. Blake checked out books, and Cassidy locked

and unlocked the door to let people out. Their remembrances match. Mrs. Blake remembers Mrs. Montgomery being there after the other library patrons left." Hogan took a drink of coffee. I started to ask another question, but he waved me into silence.

"Now it's my turn. First, I'm still trying not to make a general announcement on the cause of death until it's firm. I talked to Hart VanHorn, and the family is going along with that. So I'd appreciate it if neither of you would mention this."

We both nodded, and Hogan spoke again. "Tell me about finding that letter. In your purse."

"Hogan, I have no idea how it got there." First lie.

"How did you find it?"

"Well, I left the office early—"

"Why?"

"I just couldn't concentrate. I didn't really have a reason."

"Where did you go?"

"Down to the beach." I continued with the story I'd decided on ahead of time. I went to the beach and parked in the public area. I tossed my purse into the floor of the front seat, locked the van, and walked down to the water. When I came back to the van, the purse had fallen over, and I saw the plastic sleeve with the letter in it sticking out of the purse.

I even threw in a little uncertainty—"I don't know how long I was walking up and down the beach, but it wasn't more than half an hour." That was to show that I hadn't made the story up ahead of time. And I refrained from looking at Hogan as if I wasn't sure he would believe me.

Hogan didn't call me a liar. I guess that's the best I could say. I finished up with an apology.

"Hogan, of course I knew you were looking for that

letter, and I feel like an idiot for having it all the time. I guess I just stuffed it in my purse when we were looking for the keys—absentmindedly. I certainly did not know it was in there."

Hogan asked a few more questions. Had I left the purse unattended anytime today? Could someone else have put the letter in it? I said I didn't think so. I didn't remember any such opportunity.

Finally, Hogan rubbed his eyes. "Larry Underwood isn't going to be happy with this."

"Tough," I said. "It's my story, and I'm sticking to it." Part of me hoped I could do that, and part of me was sure I couldn't. But I had to try.

"Larry doesn't like oddball remembrances. I'd like to tell you that you're off the list of suspects, but he's not going to go for that."

"I never even met Abigail Montgomery," I said. "I had no reason to kill her."

"I know. But this letter—disappearing and reappearing—is going to make him wonder."

Hogan stood up. "Of course, you might make a better impression on Larry if you came up with some other information."

"I've told you everything I know. What other information does he want?"

"I guess you'd call it the local gossip. You know. Who got along with who. Which board members were buddy-buddy, and which ones never spoke."

"How would I know all that? I'm not even on the library board yet! I haven't had any opportunity to see how they interact."

"Well, I hear they're having a special meeting tomorrow."

"Nobody's invited me. And, besides, the library board is a public body. You can go yourself."

"You're a smart gal, Lee. It would be interesting to hear your impression of what goes on when they all get together."

"Hogan! Are you asking me to spy on the library board members?"

"Not spy, Lee. Just do your duty as a citizen." Hogan patted my shoulder. "That way I can assure Larry Underwood that you're on our side."

"Of course I'm on your side!"

"He may be a little hard to convince. I mean, he may feel that you weren't as forthcoming as you might have been over that missing letter." Hogan gave a little shrug. "Just don't let any of the board members lure you down to the cellar."

Joe walked Hogan out to his car, and I started putting pots and pans in the dishwasher. Not the cast-iron skillet, of course. I was rubbing that out with a paper towel when Joe came back inside. He leaned casually against the kitchen door.

"Okay," he said. "What's the deal on this letter Hogan was talking about?"

Chapter 10

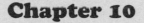

This was going to be tricky.

To be honest—so to speak—I'd pictured lying to Hogan about the letter, but I hadn't prepared myself to lie to Joe.

But what choice did I have? I could hardly tell him I fell in lust with a total stranger and on the spur of the moment decided that I'd help him lie to law enforcement authorities, including one I was related to.

So I stood there silently, continuing to scrub the remnants of chicken-fried steak out of the iron skillet, and Joe spoke again. "Why didn't you mention this, Lee? It seems sort of important."

I still didn't have an answer. So Joe tried again. "You never mentioned being a witness in a murder case. Instead we bickered about Meg Corbett—who doesn't matter a crap to us."

I shot a glance at him. Meg didn't matter a crap to us? Had all my worry been for nothing? Or was Joe lying before I could?

Joe was looking innocent. A little too innocent. Was he shading the truth?

In any case, he was still asking questions. "Why didn't you tell me about the changes in the investigation into Mrs. Montgomery's death?"

I took a deep breath and went for it. "Hogan told me not to mention it, though I suppose he didn't mean I couldn't tell you. But I guess I just didn't want to talk about it. You can see why; now Hogan wants me to spy on the members of the library board."

"That's not exactly what he asked you to do."

"It's what it amounts to."

"All he asked for was background."

"Background, my eye! He's trying to figure out who among the people at that meeting last night disliked Abigail Montgomery enough to kill her."

"That's his job."

"Yes, but it's not mine." I turned and spoke directly to Joe. "Am I sneaky enough to do that?"

"You say yourself that you're nosy enough."

"Yes, but when I try to find things out, Joe, I just ask. I don't finagle around."

"You become Mrs. Blunt? Actually, Lee, you'll do nearly anything to find stuff out, if you want to know badly enough." He grinned, but we both knew he wasn't being funny. "It's one of the things I like best about you. You've got a curiosity bump the size of a watermelon."

The argument might have grown if the phone hadn't rung right then. Joe was closer, so he picked it up, then handed it to me. It was Rhonda Ringer-Riley. And she was inviting me to a meeting of the library board.

"We're calling it for four o'clock tomorrow," she said. "That's plenty of time to comply with the open-meeting law."

All I could think of was Hogan's request. Find out

who likes whom, who dislikes whom, who always disagrees with whom.

My impulse was to tell Rhonda I couldn't come. Then she went on. "I hope you can make it, Lee. We need an outside view."

"Why?"

"We've become a rather ingrown group. Abigail was the only person who hadn't been on the board for at least five years." She laughed. "We've been through two pregnancies with Gwen!"

I took a deep breath and decided to be blunt. "Hogan wants me to go. He wants an outsider to look at the relationships among the board members."

"In relation to Abigail's death?"

"I guess so. I'd feel like a spy."

"Spy away, Lee. I don't think anybody on the board has anything to worry about. None of us know anything about Abby's accident."

I hung up without committing myself, but I kept thinking about her last comment. She didn't think anybody on the library board knew anything about what had happened to Mrs. Montgomery.

This in turn reminded me of one of Hogan's tenets: Anybody will kill if they're pushed too far.

And it also reminded me of his more recent advice: "Don't let anybody lure you to the basement."

That had been Abigail Montgomery's mistake.

I shuddered. And as I did I realized that Joe was still standing there, waiting to continue the argument about why I hadn't told him Hogan thought Abigail Montgomery's death had been a homicide, and that I was among the suspects.

And I still didn't want to tell him I didn't bring it up because I was more upset about seeing him with Meg than I was about poor Abigail being killed.

I had to fight the temptation to stamp my foot and yell, but I finally spoke fairly calmly. "I just don't want to talk about this. Okay?"

Joe seemed to awaken to the fact that I was truly upset. He took three steps toward me and put his arms around me. "It's okay, Lee. I should have understood. You took it all so calmly last night that I hadn't realized how upset you really are."

I guess the heroine of a romantic novel would have burst into tears. But all I did was hug him back. In fact, I nearly broke one of his ribs. That's because I was picturing that rib as being Meg Corbett's neck. If she got hold of Joe . . . Well, in that case I could tell Hogan exactly what event pushed me hard enough to commit murder.

Anyway, the rest of the evening and most of the next day passed—with Joe and me not talking about the things that were really on our minds. And at four o'clock on Wednesday I trailed into the Warner Pier Public Library, waved at Mrs. Blake—once again checking out books—and went back to the meeting room. And once again the only person already there was Dr. Cornwall. But this time he was awake.

"Good evening, Mrs. Woodyard," he said. "May I call you Lee?"

"Please do."

"It's a name I find interesting. During my scholarly career, I made a lengthy study of the famous general. Since you were born in a state that seceded during the Civil War, I wondered if you were named for General Robert E."

"Not directly. Lee is a common middle name for both girls and boys in Texas, and I imagine originally it may have been popular because of the general. But I was the first Lee in my family. I think my parents just liked the name."

"Then Lee is your middle name?"

"Yes. My first name is Susanna. After a pioneer great-great-great-somebody who came to Texas while it still belonged to Mexico." I smiled. "I think my mother was on some sort of Texas kick when I was born. I'm lucky I wasn't called Dallas, Austin, or Waxahachie. So I wasn't named after General Lee, but my dad did have a great-great-grandfather who served in the Texas cavalry during the Civil War. Of course, my mom had a great-grandfather who served in the Third Michigan."

"That unit campaigned in Texas. Did your ancestor get as far as San Antonio?"

"No, he was wounded at Sharpsville and went home for the rest of the war. So I'm not haunted by the specter of my great-great-great-grandfathers shooting at each other."

"Lots of Americans should be. More than most people realize."

I was quite surprised at Dr. Cornwall's friendliness. He had previously seemed quite grumpy. The opportunity to pump him seemed too good to miss, though I didn't have the nerve to start with questions about Abigail Montgomery.

I began with something innocuous. "Are you a native of Michigan?"

"No, I'm originally from Indiana. I vacationed here for years and finally became a permanent resident ten years ago."

"And where did you spend your academic career, Dr. Cornwall?"

This was meant to be an innocuous question, but his

response was not innocuous. It was almost as if I'd thrown a bomb. He glared angrily and snapped out an answer.

"I'm not Doctor Cornwall!"

My response was to gape like an idiot.

He went on, and he continued to be snappy. "I prefer to be Mr. Cornwall. Or just Corny."

"Certificate! I mean, certainly." Darn, I'd twisted my tongue into a real knot. "Mr. Cornwall it is."

Cornwall seemed to realize he'd been rude. He spoke in a more moderate tone. "I lectured on the Civil War at a small college in Indiana for thirty-five years."

Then he sat back, folded his arms, and gave a loud snort.

Naturally, we were interrupted before I could decide what to say next. Gwen Swain came bustling in, still swathed in a giant sheet of fabric that held her baby. The baby itself—I couldn't identify sex or age because of the enormous covering—peeked around to see whom Mommy was greeting.

I seized the opportunity to ask Gwen questions. Anything seemed better than continuing to try to converse with Corny Cornwall.

I started with, "What is your baby's name?" That ought to give me a hint as to sex.

"Bailey." That was no help. Luckily Gwen went on. "She's eight months old. My husband got home early today, so I didn't have to bring the other two. They're curious enough after being here last night when all the excitement started."

"But Hogan did let you go home as soon as possible last night?"

"Yes, the police were very nice. But there was a lot of excitement when Abigail was found. People were running around and saying . . . things I didn't want the kids to hear. Geraldine has been full of questions all day, and Hal's drinking it all in."

"I guess Hogan had a lot of questions for you, too."

"That Lieutenant Underwood came out to the house. He was there for half an hour. I didn't have much to tell him. I barely saw Abigail last night. We said hi as we came in."

"I didn't see her at all. In fact, I don't think I ever met her. Did you know her well?"

"Fairly well. She came to the Lakeshore Preservation meetings. In fact, she was chair of the research committee."

Mr. Cornwall's voice rumbled. "People forgot that Abigail came from a political family. And she was an expert researcher."

"Oh yes," Gwen said. "Abigail was the one who discovered that one little paragraph in the Kimbel trust, and that's what is keeping that stretch of beach undeveloped."

Mr. Cornwall's voice was gruff. "So far."

"True," Gwen said. "That battle isn't over yet. Abigail also worked hard on the library construction. She was the one who balked at approval of early payment to the contractor."

"Which," Mr. Cornwall said, "turned out to be a good thing."

This was a surprise to me. "You had trouble with the contractor for the new library?"

"No." Cornwall's tone was satisfied. "Since we declined to approve the final payment, the city had a weapon to hold over his head. So there was no problem. If Abigail hadn't been adamant that the board not approve that final payment, the city might have handed the money over. Following the contract's requirements to the letter meant there was no problem."

Gwen laughed. "This infuriated the city treasurer—until he saw what might have happened."

"Hmmm," I said. "I thought the city was in charge of the library funds."

"It is," Cornwall said. "But when a volunteer body is strongly urging a particular course of action, the city treasurer tends to pay attention. However, you're quite correct. The board's influence is unofficial."

"Except on the Vanderklomp trust," Gwen said. "We actually have a minor say on that."

"Are there other trusts benefiting the library?"

Both Gwen and Cornwall shook their heads. Then Gwen looked behind me and smiled. "And here's the expert on our finances. Hi, Carol."

Carol Turley came in, and just as she had at the previous meeting, she slammed her red leather folder down. Her hair was just as dull and lifeless as it had been earlier. Then she looked up, and her big brown eyes flashed around the room.

The old pageant contestant in me wanted to shake my head in disbelief. If Carol would just stand up straight, wear a little makeup, and do something with her hair . . .

Carol nodded to everyone, but I was the only person she spoke to by name. "Hi, Lee. I see you haven't given up on us."

"Rhonda particularly asked me to come. I guess she wants to go over exactly what happened the other night."

Carol looked around defiantly and plunked herself into a folding chair so hard I thought it was going to fold up. "I'm tired of talking about poor Abigail. The whole thing makes me sick!"

I was smart enough to keep quiet, but Gwen walked right into the buzz saw.

"But, Carol," she said, "the situation isn't going to go away until the law officers are convinced that Abigail—"

Carol slammed her fist on the table. "Abigail! Abigail! Saint Abigail! I'm sick of it. Abigail was a hard worker, but she was just a person! She was a nitpicker to end all nitpickers! I used to get so tired of her that I could barely hold my tongue. And now she's dead, and she's still causing trouble!"

With that Carol got up and walked out of the room, leaving Gwen, Mr. Cornwall, and me sitting there blankly.

"Wow!" I said. "A little pent-up resentment there, I guess."

"Not pent-up anymore," Mr. Cornwall said.

Gwen shook her head sadly, and Bailey gave a sudden cry from her sling.

"It's okay, sweetie," Gwen said soothingly. "She's just upset. People get upset. But they get over it."

Would she? Carol's reaction to Abigail's death and the investigation into it seemed extreme. Would I have to report it to Hogan?

This wasn't shaping up as a very polite meeting.

That thought had barely crossed my mind when I heard another loud voice coming from outside the meeting room. This time it was a man's voice.

"No! No, I can't allow it."

"Mr. Cassidy! I must look for some personal property!"

That voice I recognized. It was Miss Ann Vanderklomp.

"No!" And the male voice was Butch Cassidy's. "I'm responsible, Miss Vanderklomp. And you may not break the crime-scene tape and go into the basement."

Chapter 11

Gwen, Corny Cornwall, and I all jumped up and rushed out of the meeting room. Butch Cassidy sounded as if he needed all the help he could get.

The door to the back hall and basement was only a few steps away, and he and Miss Vanderklomp were nose to nose outside it. They ignored us newcomers completely.

"Mr. Cassidy," Miss Vanderklomp said. "I wish to remind you that this is the Vanderklomp Memorial Library. My family donated this building to Warner Pier, and I am accustomed to having a small say in how the institution is run."

"And I'm accustomed to staying out of jail," Butch said.

"Jail? I beg your pardon! Why would you be threatened with jail?"

"Because the authorities sealed that door, and they want it left that way. I am in charge of the library operations, so it's my responsibility to see that the door remains sealed."

"But some of my personal belongings are stored there. I must access the area."

Butch frowned. "You are a private individual. You can't use library space for personal uses."

Miss Vanderklomp took a deep breath. She seemed to fill up like a parade balloon. With her gray bob, tall stature, and blocky build, all she needed was a pair of wooden shoes to look like a giant representation of the proverbial boy who stuck his finger in the dike. I almost looked for her mooring ropes, hoping we could keep her from floating away. Or maybe cut them and let her go.

But as she expanded, she turned slightly. And she saw her audience. Apparently she hadn't noticed we were there earlier. And we deflated her.

She stepped back and seemed to become smaller. She smiled her most gracious smile and adjusted her bra straps.

"Mr. Cassidy," she said, "I do apologize. I've been making a scene about nothing. Please forgive me."

She nodded regally to Butch, then to the rest of us. And she walked into the meeting room, her head held high, clutching her water bottle.

We all followed. Mr. Cornwall raised his eyebrows, but he came along, just the same way I did. None of us asked a question or made a comment. We just went back to the meeting room.

But I sure did wonder what was in that basement. Miss Vanderklomp had already come by my office to quiz me about getting in there. Now she had apparently made a frontal attack on the underground section of the library, and Butch had barely stopped her from tearing off the crime-scene tape and invading the area.

What was down there?

As we filed in I realized that Carol had rejoined us,

and Rhonda had also arrived. We all took our seats like ladies and gentlemen, and Rhonda called the meeting to order. The only new agenda item, she said, was to review the effect the investigation into Abigail Montgomery's death would have on the library operations. She brought up two or three items the board had failed to consider on Monday, when the meeting ended rather dramatically.

Throughout the meeting I was self-consciously aware of Hogan's request that I watch how everyone interacted. I watched them all suspiciously. And I didn't notice a thing out of the ordinary.

I was relieved when Rhonda called on Butch for a report on the current situation at the library.

The investigation was having very little effect on actual operations, Butch said. "The library remained closed yesterday, but we opened on schedule this morning. Of course, we've had a busy day today. I believe Betty has issued a dozen new cards."

"The common garden-variety sensation seeker," Cornwall said.

Butch nodded. "I'm sure the curiosity effect will wear off soon. I'm also sure everyone here has been interviewed by the investigators."

Carol gave an angry sniff. "I certainly knew nothing to tell them. And I owe Corny, Gwen, and Lee an apology. I shouldn't have lost my temper when I first came in."

The three of us made "never mind" motions. Gwen was the only one who spoke. "We're all in an emotional uproar," she said. "I didn't like that detective upsetting my kids."

"I'm sure we were all cooperative," Rhonda said soothingly.

"I haven't talked to the investigators," Miss Vanderklomp said. "And I don't intend to do so."

"I'm afraid you must, if they request an interview," Rhonda said. "After all, to them we're all witnesses."

"I am not a witness! I saw nothing. I didn't even speak to Abigail Monday."

"But, Miss Vanderklomp, you and Abigail and I met on the front steps. We came in together."

"That's not speaking. That's just greeting each other. We didn't discuss anything."

I decided to jump in. "Did Mrs. Montgomery seem normal when you met her? I mean, she wasn't angry or preoccupied or anything?"

"Certainly not!"

"That's the sort of thing the detectives need to know," I said. "If she was calm, fine. But if she'd been upset or angry—"

"I didn't know her well enough to read her moods by the way she said 'hello,'" Miss Vanderklomp said. She threw her head back and looked down her nose at me.

"I am not a witness," she said, "and I am definitely not talking to any detectives. You, Mrs. Woodyard, were the person who declared Mrs. Montgomery dead. You remained with her body until the emergency technicians came. You are the one they should question."

She made her mouth into a prim little line and gave a firm nod.

I had definitely been put in my place. In fact, the whole board was in its place. And we all accepted our chastisement meekly.

"Is that all the board's business?" Miss Vanderklomp asked.

Rhonda rolled up her knitting. "I will mention that I talked to the funeral home about services for Abigail."

"Oh yes," Miss Vanderklomp said. "We should sit in a group."

"That won't be possible. The services are to be private."

Miss Vanderklomp frowned in a disapproving manner. But she left with no further comment.

But as soon as she was out of the room, Mr. Cornwall gave a rich chuckle. "What a disappointment for Ann," he said. "There's nothing she likes better than a juicy funeral."

And with that comment he followed her out the door.

Gwen spoke. "Totally wacko," she said. "All of them."

I was growing to like Gwen more all the time.

Carol gathered her papers. "Since there's no funeral, I guess we ought to go by the house."

"It sounds as if the family wants as little attention as possible," I said. "You can sign the book at the funeral home, even if there's no visitation. Or a handwritten note is always proper. And if that remark sounded incredibly prissy, it's because when I was sixteen somebody made me take an etiquette class at the YWCA."

Gwen chuckled. "Your comment may have been prissy, but the recommendation is good. I think a short note to Timothy Hart will fulfill any obligation I have."

Carol, Gwen, and I all left, and I went straight to Aunt Nettie. Not for comfort, but for advice. After all, I'm only an adopted citizen of Warner Pier. I needed to consult her about local funeral etiquette. Joe and I knew Tim pretty well. Was a note enough? Should we go to see him? Or was it better to let the family have its privacy?

I was a bit surprised when she came out in favor of a visit to Tim's home.

"Considering your rather close acquaintance with Tim," she said, "you probably should drop by."

"Oh, dear. Should I take food?"

"I don't think you need to cook anything. I'll go with you, and we'll take a box of chocolates. Is now a good time? I need to finish enrobing."

"Enrobing" always sounds to me as if the chocolatier is dressing up for a ball. Actually, the word describes giving bonbons, and sometimes truffles, a chocolate shower bath. Chocolate makers have special machines to do this.

The first step in making a bonbon is forming a shell, a hard chocolate case of the desired size and shape. These are made in utensils that look a bit like ice-cube trays. Melted chocolate is poured into them, then poured out, so that only the walls and floors are covered.

These shells are filled with fondant in the desired flavor. (My favorite is a soft, goocy Dutch caramel It has almost no resemblance to those chewy caramels that come wrapped in cellophane.) A solid chocolate lid then is used to close each shell. Ah, but the bon bon is upside down at that point. So after the lid has cooled and become solid, the chocolate maker flips it over, places it on a conveyer belt, then runs it through the enrober. The bonbon moves along a conveyer belt while melted chocolate—either white, milk, or dark—showers gently over it.

Excess chocolate falls into a receptacle underneath and is scooped up to be melted for another use; we don't waste it.

To complete the process, the bonbon is sent on a trip through the cooling tunnel, then hand decorating is added, and a bonbon has been born.

Yum.

It took Aunt Nettie about half an hour to get the enrobing process to a stopping place, then change from her white uniform into a casual pantsuit she had hanging in her locker for just such an emergency. It was five thirty when we pulled into Timothy Hart's driveway.

A uniformed security guard greeted us, so I guess Hart and his uncle were trying to avoid strangers, particularly reporters. Timothy Hart, the guard said, was receiving guests at Mrs. Montgomery's house. He pointed out where other guests had parked, and told us to join them.

The Hart compound on Lake Shore Drive is a large piece of property overlooking Lake Michigan. Tim told me once that his grandfather picked it up by paying the back taxes during the 1920s. The value of just the land today would be close to a million dollars. The houses and storage buildings would quadruple that figure.

There are four houses and a large storage barn on the land, and they almost provide a history of the property, maybe of Warner Pier as well.

Nearest the road is a small white farmhouse, probably built in the 1890s. Tim lives there. Behind it is a Craftsman bungalow. I've always assumed that Tim's grandparents built that in the twenties, soon after they acquired the property. Overlooking the lake are a brick house and a stone house. Both have low roofs and a 1970s look.

The stone house was built by Olivia VanHorn and her husband. Olivia was, of course, Tim's sister and Hart VanHorn's mother. It's been closed up since Olivia's death.

The brick house was built as a vacation place by Abigail Montgomery and her husband, and Abigail had lived there year-round since she retired and moved to Warner Pier.

A horseshoe-shaped drive accessed each house, then swung around to pass the storage building. The lane finished by returning to Lake Shore Drive. This provided one-way traffic circling the property. There was a tennis court in the center of the horseshoe.

Aunt Nettie and I went on down to the brick house and parked beside two cars that were already there. Tim greeted us at the front door. I was rather amused to see that the other guests included Warner Pier's state senator and his wife. They had brought a giant fruit basket. As a former elected official, Hart still has clout in party politics. The other couple was apparently from Grand Rapids. All of them had obviously come to see Hart, not Tim. As soon as we arrived, they got up and said good-bye. They seemed relieved to have an excuse to leave, and Tim seemed glad to see them go.

He gave a big sigh after the door shut behind them. Then he turned to us. "There's coffee in the kitchen. Come on back."

Abigail's house was furnished with antique Asian furniture and art. On a large Japanese screen over the couch, cranes pranced and postured among water plants. The screen's colors were muted by age; when I lived in Dallas I'd seen enough antique Japanese art to recognize this as the real thing. A kimono, its pattern vivid in reds and blues, was suspended on a second wall, and a collection of celadon urns was arranged on a table.

Three walls of a small adjoining room were lined with bookshelves. They actually held books. The fourth wall was of glass and overlooked Lake Michigan. Again, the decorative objects such as vases, candlesticks, and small statues were all Asian antiques.

"This house is beautiful," I said.

"Abby and her husband traveled in the Orient a lot," Tim said. "She could tell you the history of every piece of art they had collected."

He blinked. "I'm going to miss her, you know. We had dinner together nearly every evening."

Tim led the way into the kitchen, which had a homey feel. A small dining area also overlooked the lake. The chairs were upholstered with fabric featuring poppies. On the granite countertop was a fancy coffeepot that produced one cup at a time, so we each got to select a flavor.

As we were waiting for the gadget to perform, Aunt Nettie spoke. "Tim, are you exhausted?"

"Oh no. Hart has handled most of the callers. But he needed to go into Grand Rapids to arrange for . . . to arrange with the cemetery. Bill's ashes are already there, so Abby's will be there, too. I haven't had to do much except sit around here and wonder. I just can't understand why something like this could happen to Abby."

Neither Aunt Nettie nor I had any answer for that question. But I did seize the opportunity to ask a question of my own.

"Tim, that night at the library, you said something about Mrs. Montgomery being worried. Did you tell Hogan about that?"

"I guess I forgot to. But I didn't know what she was worried about, so it didn't seem to matter."

Tim opened the refrigerator and bent over. "I think there's some cream in here. Oh no!"

"What's wrong?" I asked.

"Hart and I asked the maid to clean out the refrigerator—you know, get rid of the perishable stuff. She hasn't touched a thing, and she went home an hour ago."

"I can do that," I said. "I already told Hart I'd be glad to help out. Do you want the things taken to your house?"

"No, I'm going to Grand Rapids, probably for at least a week. I hoped the maid would just take them away with her."

"Lee and I will be glad to clear it out," Aunt Nettie said. "We'll leave the mustard and mayonnaise, but we'll take anything that might spoil."

"I hate to ask you to do something like that."

Aunt Nettie and I assured Tim we were just being neighborly, and the three of us sat at the table and talked. Aunt Nettie encouraged Tim to reminisce about his childhood, and I was glad to see that Tim felt he could be informal with us.

Abby, he said, had always been the curious child in the family. "Once she got in trouble for going through our mother's checkbook. She said she wanted to know how much the grocery bill was."

After about twenty minutes the phone rang. As Tim went to answer it, Aunt Nettie and I found a grocery sack in a holder in the broom closet. Then we began to pack up the refrigerator.

Of course, with only one person living in the house, it wasn't exactly full anyway. We left the condiments and canned fruit alone and put the lunch meat in the freezer. We put half a dozen eggs, a quart of milk, and half a carton of cottage cheese in our sack. Then I opened the hydrator and began to hand out vegetables.

"It looks as if Abigail was quite a salad eater," I said. "Here's an unopened bag of romaine."

"We'd better take that," Aunt Nettie said. "It spoils so quickly."

I gave her tomatoes, green onions, and half a jicama. Then I reached for a head of iceberg lettuce. It was at the back of the drawer and had been stuffed into a plastic bag. The bag had been closed with a twist tie.

As soon as I picked it up, I realized it felt funny.

"Huh?" I stood up. "This is odd."

"Lettuce?"

"I don't think so," I said. I placed the head of lettuce on the counter, untwisted the wire holding its sack closed, and dumped out the contents.

The head of iceberg was made of plastic.

"Aunt Nettie," I said, "this is one of those hiding places. It's hollow. I've seen them in catalogs. You know, 'Hide your jewelry; fox the burglars.'"

Now that we had the fake lettuce out of the bag, we could see how it opened. We left it closed.

"We'll give this to Tim," Aunt Nettie said firmly.

Luckily, Tim joined us within a minute, and we showed him the plastic lettuce head.

"We'd better open it," Tim said. "It's probably my grandmother's wedding ring."

Tim's guess was right. A small velvet drawstring bag popped out of the lettuce. It held three rings, each with colored stones, and a brooch in the shape of a rose. The brooch was centered with what appeared to be a nice diamond.

"That's what I thought," Tim said. "Abby occasionally wore these, but I'm sure any other jewelry she owned is in her safety-deposit box. We found the bank box information in her desk, but we haven't had time to go down there. Wait a minute. There's something else in here."

He turned the little velvet bag upside down and shook out one final item.

A key clanked onto the granite countertop.

Chapter 12

It was a pretty key, just about three inches long. Gold in color and delicate-looking, it might have been hung in a nook as a decorative accent, or pictured on the cover of a book with a title like *The Key to Her Heart*.

When Joe and I took over the TenHuis family house, we found a half dozen keys like these—same shape, but larger—in a box in the basement. Aunt Nettie said they had been the house's original 1904 door keys.

But why on earth was this key hidden with Abigail's jewelry?

"It can't be for this house," Tim said.

Aunt Nettie agreed with him. "It's a key to a much older lock than this house would have," she said. "This house isn't more than forty years old. In fact, I'd expect this key to open a cedar chest or some sort of cabinet, not a door."

"I can't think of anything like that around here," Tim said. "Hart and I haven't taken any kind of inventory yet, but we looked around."

I picked the key up and looked closely at it. Again, I was impressed by what a delicate little piece of equipment it was. The part that hung down, the tab that actually would trip the workings of a lock, was intricately cut. It looked as if it ought to be antique, but it was shiny and new.

"Tim," I said, "your house is older than this house."

"More than a hundred years old."

"Could this key be for some lock at your house?"

"Nothing much locks at my house." Tim produced a modern door key from his pocket. "No, Abigail re-keyed this whole house when she moved back from California, and I got new locks and keys at the same time. I don't have keys anything like this one, and I never have."

We considered several other possibilities. Tim said that a key for the big storage shed, where the family's sports and garden equipment was stored, was hung on a nail in Abby's pantry. He pulled it out, and, again, that was a modern key. Plus, Tim said he was sure that Abby had had no key to the older house, the Craftsman-style their grandparents had built. "Nobody's used it since our parents died," he said. "There are two keys for it in a cupboard in my kitchen. They're nothing like this little thing."

We all stared at the key. Inspiration did not strike any of us.

"Maybe it's to Abigail's jewelry box," Aunt Nettie said.

Tim shook his head. "The jewelry box was unlocked, and the key was inside. Abigail didn't have much good jewelry." He gestured at the items we'd found in the fake lettuce. "This may be the whole collection. As I said, anything else would be in her safety-deposit box."

"One of life's little mysteries," I said. "The key is probably for something in Mrs. Montgomery's house in California, and she was keeping it as a souvenir."

"But why did she keep it with Grandma's jewelry?" Tim put the rings, the brooch, and the key back into the fake lettuce. "I'll take all this up to my house."

At that Aunt Nettie and I left, carting along the eggs and the vegetables. I was glad to go. By then it was six thirty, and I knew Joe was likely to be home. I was eager to see him. I always am.

But when Aunt Nettie and I pulled into our drive—she'd left her car there—there was no truck sitting in Joe's parking place. I felt disappointed, but not too surprised. Joe had gone to his office in Holland that afternoon, and he often runs late.

Aunt Nettie insisted that I keep the food we'd brought from Abigail's house. As she drove away, she lowered her car window and called out to me. "Hogan sent you a message, and I forgot to give it to you."

"What was it?"

"He said he's relying on you for the inside poop. I don't know what he meant."

Unfortunately, I did. I went in the house, feeling like a failure. I'd merely stumbled around, trying to figure out the personal dynamics of the library board. My questions had been useless. I hadn't learned a thing.

Joe. Maybe Joe would encourage me.

But when I got inside, the telephone answering machine was flashing, and the message was from Joe. "Sorry, Lee, but I have to stay in Holland for dinner. I should be home by nine. Or ten."

Another kick in the stomach.

Joe didn't say why he had to have dinner in Holland. No excuses. No explanations. What was I to think but the worst?

Mechanically, I began to put the things I'd brought from Abigail's house into my refrigerator. I looked at Abigail's eggs and wondered if I should scramble a couple, put on my pajamas, and turn on HGTV. An evening to veg out and feel sorry for myself sounded good.

I don't think I've ever felt as blue in my life. My Texas grandma would have said I was ready to cut my suspenders and go straight up.

Instead I went out and picked up two single guys.

Not that I did that deliberately. But Abigail's eggs didn't look appealing. Eggs are better with English muffins, and I didn't have any in the house. That was enough justification for going out to eat.

So there, Joe Woodyard.

After all, I reminded myself, I lived in a community that had good restaurants, even when the tourist season was over. I combed my hair, redid my makeup, and headed for Herrera's. It was pure coincidence that I ran into Butch Cassidy and Corny Cornwall having dinner together there.

When I came in they were still at the martini stage and hadn't ordered dinner yet. Mr. Cornwall invited me to join them.

I assured myself that I wasn't sneaking around. After all, Herrera's belongs to my husband's stepfather, and even if Mike isn't there, he hears about who comes in. So the word would get back to Joe, even if I didn't tell him about it. Which I planned to do. I spread my napkin over my lap and ordered a glass of pinot noir.

Of course, simmering right under my consciousness was the knowledge that I was having dinner with a man to whom I was strongly attracted and that he'd shown some signs that he was attracted to me.

Or was that my imagination?

"Cheers," Butch said. He lifted his martini toward me, and our eyes met.

No, it wasn't my imagination. We both looked away quickly.

I focused my attention on the older man. "Dr. Cornwall . . . oh, I'm sorry! I haven't forgotten that you prefer to be called mister."

"I wish you could bring yourself to call an old man Corny," he said.

"Of course, if that's what you prefer, Corny."

"I wasn't very polite about my title this afternoon, and I'd like to explain. It's all Abigail's fault."

"How?"

"At the college where I taught for most of my academic career, somehow I got grandfathered in. I was the only faculty member in the history department who never received a doctorate. It's unbelievable by today's standards." He leaned closer and smiled. "All I have is an ABD."

I grinned back. "All but Dissertation?"

"Right. I finished off all the requirements for my doctorate and I wrote the dissertation, but I never got it through the idiotic committee. Which changed four times."

"You mean the committee changed?"

"Yes. The personnel on the committee. Of course, each group wanted a different approach to the material. New research. After five years, I told the dean he'd just have to fire me. I wasn't going to fool with it anymore, even if I had to teach in high school again."

"Apparently the dean didn't take you at your word."

"No. He kept me on semester to semester for a while. Then I became one of the only permanent faculty members without a doctorate. A couple of new administrations tried to oust me. But none of them succeeded." He smiled wickedly. "The alumni loved me. They got together and endowed a chair to be held only by me. I even received an honorary doctorate when I retired."

"Then you are entitled to be called doctor."

"It would be only a courtesy title. I prefer simply to be Corny. The situation didn't seem to matter until I retired to Warner Pier. People I met here began to call me doctor. I corrected them for a while, but it called for long explanations. I finally just let it go."

"How did Abigail Montgomery affect the situation?"

Corny sipped his martini. "The damn woman was a hell of a researcher. I admit that."

"Oh! She discovered the history of your academic title."

"Don't ask me how. Or why she bothered. But all of a sudden I was getting these innuendoes about my academic career. From her."

"How annoying!"

"That's a good word. 'Annoying.'"

"It seems pointless," I said. "Unless she wanted money or something else valuable to keep quiet."

"No! She never seemed to want to gain any advantage with her knowledge. It embarrassed me, but not seriously. It didn't cost me a job or break up a love affair or anything. I found her actions a great mystery."

At that point the waiter came with our salads. The break in conversation recalled me to my manners. Since the moment I sat down, Corny and I had done all the talking. It was time to include Butch. But I wanted to continue to focus on Abigail.

"Butch, did you ever meet Abigail?"

"Only once." He nodded to Corny. "At that interview meeting with the board. She gave me the same treatment she gave you, Corny. She'd done more research on my personal life than I was comfortable with. Not my professional life. She was certainly entitled to look that over thoroughly. But she had found out things about my past I didn't want to discuss. Frankly, I'm a little relieved to hear you say that she treated someone else that way."

"I noticed she made several people on the library board uncomfortable." Corny stabbed a piece of tomato. "I finally decided there was nothing malicious in it."

"I thought perhaps she was trying to gain power," Butch said. "Emotional power."

"If she was, she never seemed to use it."

I waved my own salad fork around. "But people cited examples of when she influenced board action. Halting the payment on parts of the building, for example. Not that that wasn't a good thing to do."

"Abigail never seemed to use her nosiness to put pressure on people," Corny said. "I mean, she was quite open about things she wanted. She cited chapter and verse. Abigail was curious, but she didn't appear mean."

Butch leaned forward and spoke in a low voice. "Corny, do you know of any run-in Abigail had with Betty Blake?"

"Betty? The circulation-desk clerk? No, I don't."

"There seems to be bad feeling there."

"Over what?"

Butch shook his head. "I've probably said too much."

That was interesting. Maybe it was something Hogan ought to know about.

We left the subject then. It seemed to be time to talk about something besides Abigail Montgomery.

So Corny and I described a few of Warner Pier's traditional events to Butch, starting with the Fall Rinky-dink and the midwinter tourism promotion.

The Rinkydink marks the day our one traffic light is turned into a blinking light for the winter. We all get together for a benefit picnic lunch in our waterfront park. Then we cheer the city crew as they switch the light over.

The midwinter promotion has a different theme every year, and that year the theme was to be clowns. Butch liked that idea. He immediately had some great ideas about projects the library could do involving clowns. I was impressed with his imagination.

But I kept thinking about Betty Blake disliking Abigail. If I was checking out a book, Betty seemed to be the most docile person in the world. The idea that she could even get mad—and mad at one of the library board members—was a surprise.

Butch and Corny—I was getting used to calling him that—were good company, and it turned out to be a pleasant evening.

Until we all got up to leave. That's when those questions about Joe surfaced again in my little brain. Why hadn't he come home for dinner? And whom was he having dinner with? Should I worry? Or was I simply borrowing trouble?

Corny had had three martinis, so I was glad to learn he lived only a block away from Herrera's. Butch—he and I had each had only one drink—offered to walk home with him, and the two of them escorted me to my van. This meant Butch and I had no opportunity for private conversation.

Which was a good thing. We were doing well enough with eye contact alone. He did touch my arm as I got in the van. I pretended not to notice.

"Good night," Corny said. "It's been a long day."

"Long for me, too," I said. "I'm ready for bed." The parking lot was not well lit. I hoped Butch couldn't see that my face got hot. And why should a routine remark like that embarrass me?

As I drove home I grew more depressed by the moment. Where was Joe? Had he been with Meg? Were we having a crisis? Was I all excited over nothing?

Joe's truck was in its proper spot when I pulled into the drive. I didn't know if I should feel happy or angry or full of dread. I took a deep breath and went in the house.

Joe met me at the kitchen door. We spoke in unison. "Where've you been?"

And we answered in unison. "Out to dinner."

Then the conversation seemed to flag. "Good," I said finally. "You've eaten. Where did you go?"

"Oh, just down the street to Pepe's. Webb and I had a case we wanted to talk about."

A load lifted from my shoulders. Webb Bartlett is one of Joe's fellow lawyers. In fact, he founded the agency where Joe works, though he maintains a private practice and rarely gets involved in their cases. But it certainly wasn't unusual for Joe and Webb to confer.

"How is Webb?" I asked.

"Oh, he's fine. Where'd you go?"

"I'm now on a nickname basis with Corny Cornwall." I described my dinner. Maybe I downplayed Butch Cassidy, just a little bit. But I didn't fudge the facts.

"And earlier," I said, "Aunt Nettie and I cleaned out Abigail Montgomery's refrigerator."

I reported on that visit as well, ending with a description of the mysterious key.

"Odd," Joe said. "Did the key look like a genuine antique or a copy?"

"It looked new and shiny."

"The only place to get a key copied in Warner Pier is the hardware store. Guy Reardon might remember if Mrs. Montgomery brought a key in to be copied."

"Should I mention this to Hogan? Or let Tim handle it?"

"Tim or Hart ought to tell Hogan, I guess. Or maybe all of us should just forget it."

I had hoped my detailed story about my day would encourage Joe to give me a bit more detail about his. But no such report was forthcoming. We seemed to run out of conversation. Joe wandered around, and after a few minutes got into the shower. And I turned to HGTV, just as I had threatened earlier in the evening. We both climbed in bed early, but we each brought reading material with us. The only communication was, "What time shall I set the alarm for?"

Of course, by then it had occurred to me that if Joe had a problem—such as an old girlfriend—that he wanted to discuss with a trusted adviser, Webb would have been a likely candidate for the role. So I propped up on my pillows, held my book, and didn't read it. It was one o'clock before I turned out my light, and then I didn't sleep well.

The next morning I got up determined to finish up the chore Hogan had requested so I could concentrate on my own life. Betty Blake was my next victim, I decided.

Butch had said she had some problem with Abigail. I needed to find out what it was. I considered several ways to accomplish this and finally decided I should just ask her. As soon as I got to the office I found Betty's home phone number and called her. She readily agreed to meet me for lunch. I told her I wanted to discuss day-to-day operations at the library.

"Well, I know all about that," she said firmly. "Though you might not think so, judging by the amount of attention I get."

Chocolate Chat

Food Network Magazine did a special issue on chocolate, and one of their articles was on chocolate-covered everything.

The magazine's test cooks tempered semisweet and milk chocolate, then dipped dozens of foods in the yummy coatings.

The items that made the cut and were pictured in the magazine included:

Shredded wheat biscuits

Dried apples

Corn chips

Saltines and cheese crackers

Melba toast

Banana chips

Red licorice

Fruits, including orange sections and grapes

Toaster waffles

And—ta-da!—fried bacon

Chapter 13

And just what did Betty mean by that? I needed to find out. That was why we were going to have a talk.

It was a beautiful fall day, so I suggested meeting at the outside area of the Sidewalk Café.

The Sidewalk actually takes its name from the décor—which includes old outdoor toys such as scooters, roller skates, jacks, and marbles—but it has both indoor and outdoor dining rooms. It's only a block from TenHuis Chocolade, and everybody in town walks by. It even has good food. It's the most popular place in Warner Pier for lunch.

To my surprise, Betty hesitated. "Maybe someplace more private would be better," she said. "I know! I'll make us a sandwich, and we can go to Riverside Park."

Hmmm. Warner Pier has a lovely park that runs beside the Warner River for several blocks. Right in downtown Warner Pier. But Betty wasn't talking about that park. She was suggesting a park that's rather hard to get to and has few amenities. Its main attraction is a boat ramp, and it's up the river, a mile from downtown Warner Pier. Why did she want to go there?

But it was okay with me. "That might be a better place to talk," I said. "There's never anybody there."

"That's right. We shouldn't run into anybody we don't want to see us together."

Hmmm again. Why did she want our talk to be secret?

I offered to pick up some of the Sidewalk's roast beef sandwiches and grab soft drinks from the shop's refrigerator. Betty said she had some homemade cookies. We agreed to meet at eleven thirty, since Betty went to work at one.

"This is the afternoon for the after-school movie," she said. "So I'll have to be right on time so I can help Gwen get ready."

I knew Gwen Swain was the volunteer who ran that activity.

I knew very little about Betty, so I quizzed Aunt Nettie, who rarely leaves the shop but still seems to know everybody in town. Aunt Nettie called to Nadine Vanderhill, one of the "hairnet ladies," the genius cooks who actually make TenHuis chocolates. Aunt Nettie told me Nadine went to the same church Betty did.

Nadine is a cheerful gal—tall and blond and a bit husky, like most of us descendants of the original Dutch settlers of Western Michigan.

"Why do you need to know about Betty?" Nadine asked. "She doesn't have any new problems, does she?"

I explained that I had been asked to serve on the board of the library and was trying to familiarize myself with its personnel and operations. I said nothing about getting together with Betty, since she apparently didn't want that known.

"I'm just being nosy," I said. "Betty seems to be a very nice person."

"Oh, she is!" Nadine said. "But she's had a lot of problems. Her husband went off and left her with two kids. One of the kids has needed speech therapy and tutoring and other things. You know, extra time and expense. And Betty's house is old. She's had lots of problems there. She's just never been able to get ahead."

"How old are her kids?"

"Early twenties. Her daughter works at a nursing home in Holland, and her son is at Walmart in South Haven. He got married just out of high school and had kids right away. So now it's more problems with the grandkids."

"It sounds as if Betty has had a hard life."

"Lots of troubles. The church has tried to help Betty, but she's had a struggle. I think she's a real hard worker. And she's smart. Through it all she's kept on taking college classes."

"That can be hard," I said. "I worked full-time while I went to college. It wasn't easy, and I didn't have kids."

"I think Betty finally finished her degree last spring. Maybe things will look up for her."

Armed with two roast beef sandwiches and a few facts about Betty, I headed for lunch. When I pulled into Riverside Park an old sedan was already there, and I saw Betty sitting at a picnic table.

There was nothing very distinctive about her. She looked like a middle-aged woman. She had a round face, pale eyelashes, and mouse brown hair styled with a bad perm. She wore shapeless slacks, a baggy shirt, and run-over loafers. She probably needed to lose thirty pounds. To be honest, duplicates of Betty Blake can be found in any American supermarket.

When I joined her at the table, her expression was worried.

"I hope there's nothing wrong," she said.

Nothing except a murder, I thought. But I didn't say that. What I said was, "I just wanted to understand the library's day-to-day operations." Betty still looked wary.

We each took a sandwich and a Diet Coke. Between bites, Betty described her work at the Warner Pier Public Library. The staff totaled six, she reported. Butch Cassidy, of course, was the director. Betty had the title assistant librarian, and there were four others classified as clerks. Betty and the other four watched the desk, shelved the books, helped the patrons find materials, and did clerical chores from ten a.m. until seven or eight p.m. Monday through Saturday, working staggered shifts. In the past the library director had taken a shift on the circulation desk, and Butch had indicated he planned to continue this. Betty was the staff member who posted the bills and kept track of the fines, then sent these figures to the director, who passed them on to the city treasurer. The library shared a custodian with another city office, and he came in at night.

I didn't ask about the basement, since I wasn't trying to investigate the death of Abigail. No, my purpose was to understand the personal dynamics of the people who had been in the library building when Abigail died. But Betty did volunteer some information on the basement. The area, she said, was used only for storage. The night she stumbled over Abigail's body, she had gone down to get paper for the copy machine.

"I'll never forget that," she said. "It was horrible!"

I made sympathetic noises and moved on to another subject.

"How long have you worked at the library?"

"Eighteen years," Betty said. "I'm the employee with the longest service. But it's a very small operation. I don't understand why they decided to hire a *professional* librarian."

Betty definitely had given the word "professional" a special meaning, and it wasn't a complimentary one.

"Wasn't Mrs. Smith a professional librarian?" I asked.

"No. She had a degree in English. Just like me. But the library board decided to replace her with someone with a master's of library science."

"Was that because of the new library building? I mean, did they want a more professional operation?"

"It's the same library! I don't see why a new building should make a difference! It will have the same books, the same computers, the same Internet access that the old one has!"

"Is the budget increasing?"

"Somewhat." The word came out grudgingly.

Obviously this whole topic was a sore one to Betty Blake. I simply made a noncommittal sound. "Hmmm."

That was enough encouragement for Betty. She went on. "So they hired this man, Mr. Cassidy. He has an MLS. But his library experience is practically nil!"

"Oh? The newspaper story said he'd worked in libraries for several years."

"Yes, while he was in graduate school. He checked out books in a city library, a very low-level job, then worked at the University of Michigan library. But a college library is quite different from a community library. I'm sure Mr. Cassidy knows about handling orders for books requested by professors, or helping students research esoteric topics. But he's never planned programs for children. Or organized a teen book club. Or helped tourists check their e-mail. Or even worked on the Friends of the Library book sale. He's nice enough, I guess, but he's not experienced in the type of operation we have here in Warner Pier."

Betty ducked her head. "I can't help feeling—cheated. Oh, I shouldn't have said that!"

"I won't pass anything along you say."

I might as well have kept quiet. Betty wanted to talk, and I was the first person who had offered to listen to her.

"It's just that Catherine—Mrs. Smith—well, she promised me that once I got my degree and she retired, I would be in line to be considered for the position. Then that Mrs. Montgomery, well, she came up with that plan to 'upgrade.' That's what she called it. She wanted to hire a 'professional' librarian."

"I see."

"She pushed the budget changes through with the vice mayor. Then she pushed her plan through the library board. So here I am. I worked all these years for my degree, and it was no use!"

I tried to make soothing noises, but I could see how futile my efforts were. Betty had hoped to follow Mrs. Smith as director of the Warner Pier Public Library. She had worked hard, not only at her job, but at her education. And as a single mother in a low-paying job, this would have been a struggle. Then, just as she attained her bachelor's degree, the game changed. The library board decided to hire someone with a master's.

I could understand her feelings entirely. But I could also understand the board's desire to call for higher qualifications for the director.

All I could do was cluck sympathetically, but noncommittally.

Luckily, once she had her grievance off her chest,

Betty seemed to feel a little better. "Everyone was sympathetic," she said. "I talked to Miss Vanderklomp. But she said that she's not an official member of the board. Of course, she forgets that when she wants to. If she'd been on my side . . . And Mrs. Ringer-Riley was highly sympathetic, but she didn't support me either.

"So here I am, with a useless degree."

"Oh, Betty, all that work! You can't regard it as useless."

"I enjoyed the classes. I like to learn, and I love English literature."

"So it wasn't a waste of effort. And you don't have to work at the Warner Pier library forever. Have you tried Holland? Or one of the other library systems?"

"I'd have to start at the bottom there. And I can't look too far away from Warner Pier because I really can't afford to move. I inherited my house from my parents, and I owned it mortgage free until I had to borrow money for repairs. And the city has good benefits! My daughter is still on my insurance."

I hadn't thought about benefits. Jobs around Warner Pier are not easy to find unless the job seeker is in certain categories. And by joining with other small municipalities, the city is able to offer a nice benefit package. A person with the problems Betty had had would find that attractive.

On the other hand, property is worth quite a bit in Warner Pier. Even if Betty's house needed repairs . . .

I opened my mouth, then shut it without saying anything. Betty hadn't asked me for financial guidance. A lot of Joe's clients are in deep financial doo-doo, so if she did ask for advice, Joe could help her find an adviser. But it wasn't my place to make suggestions on how Betty handled her money. Or suggest that she quit her job and move elsewhere.

Betty and I seemed to have reached the end of our conversation. But I had one more question.

"Betty," I said, "why didn't you want anyone to know we were meeting for lunch?"

Betty turned as red as one of Michigan's prize apples. "Oh, I didn't want to hide anything!"

"But you said that you preferred to meet here, rather than at the Sidewalk Café, because then we wouldn't see anyone we didn't want to see us together."

"Oh! Did I say that? I didn't mean anything by it. I just didn't want anyone to think I was talking out of school. I guess I thought you might want to talk about something a little touchier."

"Like what? What's touchy about the library? Other than Abigail Montgomery being killed, of course."

"Oh, but that has nothing to do with the library!"

"It happened there."

"But it must have been an accident! I'm sure it was."

I shut up again. Hogan hadn't announced that he believed Abigail's death had been caused deliberately. I wasn't supposed to know that, much less spread it around.

"Anyway," Betty went on, "I'll be glad to discuss the library anytime. The everyday operations. The finances. Anything. Just call me."

I assured her that I appreciated her information.

Having confided in me—human nature being what it is—Betty was now regretting what she'd said. And I was a bit embarrassed that I'd encouraged her to tell me her secrets. We said good-bye a little stiffly and gathered up our sacks, paper napkins, and Coke cans to put them in the proper bins. I thanked Betty effusively for giving me an inside look at the library from a staffer's viewpoint.

She smiled wistfully. "It's so nice to see a board

member really take an interest in the library," she said. "Most of them just seem to swallow whatever the director tells them."

Her comment made me feel a bit guilty. If Hogan hadn't instructed me to look into the interactions of the board members, well, I'd have been a board member who just swallowed whatever the director told me.

I drove away, wondering. Had I learned anything from Betty?

Yes, I decided.

First, some people had said that Abigail Montgomery was negligible as a member of the library board, that she didn't take an active part in the organization's business. Apparently that wasn't correct. According to Betty, Abigail had been the big pusher in the effort to upgrade the qualifications of the library director. She had gotten Butch Cassidy his job.

Hmm. Had she and the other supporters of the upgrade had Butch in mind for the job all along? This has been known to happen. Had one or more of them known him earlier? Or had they been genuinely convinced that the Warner Pier Public Library should have a director with an MLS, and Butch happened to be the best-qualified applicant?

I decided that I wanted to find out. Who could I ask?

How about the president of the board, Rhonda Ringer-Riley?

I pulled my van into a handy parking lot, looked up Rhonda's phone number on my cell phone, and called her. Her answering machine promised she'd call me back.

I left my number and clicked my phone off, then drove on. Until I heard from Rhonda, I could do nothing about the library. I realized I was sorry I couldn't talk to her immediately. It was so much better to worry about the death of Abigail Montgomery than to worry about Joe and Meg getting together. Once I put the library out of my mind, that problem settled on my shoulders like a portable fog.

I drove back to the office and spent a miserable hour staring at my computer, not thinking about the accounts it displayed, wishing I could go home and curl up in a ball, and being determined not to do that. No, whatever the threat to my life—love life, personal life, married life—I couldn't fight it by quitting.

But how could I fight Meg? What weapon did I have to use against her past, against Joe's past? Whatever happened between them back in high school still haunted Joe. How could I break that pattern?

I was worrying so hard that when the phone rang I nearly fell off my chair.

"Lee? It's Betty."

For a moment I couldn't think of who I knew named Betty. My answer must have sounded completely blank. "Yes?"

"I was looking through my financial files, Lee, because I needed to post the latest bills. I've run across something really odd. Could I talk to you about it?"

Now I knew who it was. Betty Blake, of course. "Sure," I said. "What is it?"

"Probably nothing. But I can't talk now. Gwen's setting up for the movie, and I need to help her. Could you drop by here after work?"

"Of course. But what's the problem?"

"It's not a problem exactly. It's just something odd. You'll probably be able to explain it right away."

"I'll be there around five."

"Thanks." She hung up.

What was all that about?

At four forty-five I gave up trying to work and

walked the three blocks to the library. The place was rocking. The reading room had been turned into a TV viewing area, and about twenty-five kids were watching some Disney flick. It was hard to tell which was noisier, the kids or the movie.

A half dozen people were lined up at the circulation desk. One of them was Tony Herrera Jr., who is sort of my nephew, being the son of Joe's stepbrother and my friend Lindy. He's a good-looking guy of thirteen. We gave each other a casual wave.

"Hi, Tony." I gestured at the sheaf of photocopies he was holding. "Working on a report?"

"Yeah. I'm ready to go home, as soon as Alicia gets out of the movie, but I gotta pay for my copies, and there's nobody here to take my money."

The teenaged girl in line ahead of him gave a deep sigh. "Where did Mrs. Blake disappear to? I'm going to be late to work if I don't get these books checked out."

"That's funny," I said. "Mrs. Blake is so conscientious. Isn't there anyone else around?"

"That new guy was here a little while ago," Tony said. "I'll look in his office."

I went to the back of the building. The door to the director's office was closed. When I knocked, Butch's baritone answered. "Come in."

My stomach fluttered, but I pretended it hadn't and opened the door. I asked Butch if he knew where Betty was, explaining that she seemed to have disappeared.

"Odd," Butch said, getting up. "I can fill in. But I wonder where Betty is."

"I'll look upstairs. Maybe she's been treed by an irate patron and is stuck on top of one of the stacks."

Butch laughed and headed toward the circulation desk.

I glanced up and down the aisles of the downstairs

and walked through the staff workroom. When I peeked out the back door I saw that the basement was still sealed. Then I went back into the main room and climbed the stairway to the second floor, home of adult books.

At first, the whole floor appeared to be deserted. Where could Betty have gone? Had she left the building? Why would she ask me to come over, then not be there?

I walked through the shelves, looking over sections for mysteries and science fiction. No Betty. Then I ventured into general fiction—everything from Cervantes to Elinor Glyn—and moved toward nonfiction.

When I reached the back corner I gave an enormous gasp. I almost screamed.

One of the shelving units had fallen over, landing so that it was propped against the outside wall. All the books had tumbled out and were lying heaped on the floor.

And a pair of shoes was sticking out from under the books.

Chapter 14

I guess I kept my head. I pulled out my phone and called 9-1-1. Then I did something that might seem cold-blooded: I took a quick photo of the scene with my phone. Next, I ran to the stairway, wanting to get attention from someone downstairs.

I couldn't yell for Butch, who was still standing at the desk, because of the noise from the movie and the children. Luckily, Tony was still in line, and I was able to catch his attention. I pointed to Butch and motioned that he should come upstairs.

I ran back to Betty, and again I used my phone to take a picture of the scene. I wanted to get the books off of Betty, but I knew Hogan would want to see the scene as I had originally found it.

These were a lot of different activities, but I don't think more than a minute went by between the time I first saw Betty and the time when I crawled under the leaning bookshelf and began to haul books off her motionless body.

The shoes had immediately told me Betty was the person under the books. They were the same run-over loafers she'd been wearing when we met for lunch.

Tony, as curious as any kid, ran upstairs to see what was going on. I tried to block his view of those horrible feet, and I sent him back down to wait at the front door and show the EMTs where to come. I had some vague hope that having a job would keep him away from the scene and, maybe, from being traumatized.

Of course, the 9-1-1 operator had wanted to follow the usual procedure and keep me on the line, but I told her if she had the EMTs on the way I was hanging up. I stuck the phone in my pocket, and I kept tossing books aside. In a few minutes Butch came upstairs, looking puzzled. As soon as he saw what had happened, he also began to dig through the books, throwing them behind him.

The EMTs and the Warner Pier patrolman got there within ten minutes. They made us move away from the fallen shelf, of course; I think they were afraid that it would slip and knock more shelves over. They didn't want more victims.

Hogan also came quickly. He suggested that Butch and I make lists of the people present downstairs. "Just the adults," he said. "And don't try to keep people here. It's better for that mob of kids to leave."

When we went down the movie had ended, and the children were louder than ever. Gwen asked me what had happened, and I whispered a quick explanation. She offered to help with the lists of names. Butch furnished each of us with paper and pencil. Then he announced to the whole room that there had been an accident upstairs and suggested that everybody leave. But he would like to have the adults' names, he said, just in case witnesses were needed later.

I don't think I would have gotten away with that, but Butch had that authoritative voice. All those moms and grandmas and babysitters and kids obeyed him. There were two or three other patrons there as well, including Corny Cornwall. Corny offered to stay and help, but Butch told him it wasn't necessary. After fifteen or twenty minutes no one was left but Gwen and her two kids, and Tony. His younger sister was waiting in front of the library.

I thanked Tony for helping out. He looked upset, of course. "Lee, was there someone under those books?"

"I'm afraid so, Tony. The EMTs are getting her out now."

"I guess she's dead."

"I'm afraid she is, Tony."

"I guess it's Mrs. Blake."

I nodded and took his hand. Even a step-aunt can't hug a thirteen-year-old boy in public. "It's terribly sad, and you've helped a lot."

"I better get Alicia home," he said. He walked out with his head high. I was proud of him. Then I called his mom and told her what had happened and how Tony had been involved. She promised to be ready for emotional storms.

When Tony had asked about Betty Blake, I had told him the truth. By then I felt certain that Betty was dead. If there had been any signs of life, the EMTs would have been rushing her to the hospital, but no gurney had been carried down the stairs. A few minutes later the portable crime lab operated by the Michigan State Police arrived, and I gave up any hope for her.

I turned back to Gwen and Butch. We looked at each other and took deep breaths.

Gwen was frowning. "Did you say a shelf fell over? And all the books fell out?"

"That's what it looked like," Butch said. "It must have made quite a rumble. Did you hear anything?"

"No! Of course, this movie was loud."

"I guess that was it," Butch said. "I didn't hear anything either."

"What a weird accident," Gwen said. She collected her kids—the baby had stayed home that day—and left.

As she went out, Rhonda Ringer-Riley came in. It was the first time I'd ever seen her without her knitting bag.

She shook hands with Butch and nodded to me.

"Goodness gracious!" she said. "Another disaster. What a run of bad luck."

I almost laughed. Yeah, murder can be awfully unlucky.

Then I felt sick. Both Gwen and Rhonda assumed Betty's death was an accident. I assumed that it wasn't.

Of course, I said nothing. Although Butch and I assured Rhonda that she didn't need to stay, she didn't leave. "I guess I'd better act as if I'm the board chair," she said.

So we waited. I called and left a message for Joe, explaining what had happened. I guess I hoped he'd run right down to the library to hold my hand, but that didn't happen. In a while Hogan came down, asked Butch and me for preliminary statements, and told us we could go home. Butch said he would stay and close the building, but Rhonda and I didn't need a second suggestion. We were out the door immediately. We both stopped on the sidewalk.

"Whew!" Rhonda said. "What a mess!"

"It's a nightmare. I liked Betty."

"So did I." Rhonda turned to me. "Oh. You called me

this afternoon, but I didn't get a chance to return your call."

"It seemed important at the time, but now . . ." Actually, I did still want to know. "I was wondering if any particular board member, or board members, had pushed for the hiring of Butch."

Rhonda looked troubled. "It wouldn't do much good for a board member to do that. The city personnel director did the screening and the formal interviews."

"Oh? I thought the board interviewed the finalists."

"Yes, we did. But our vote was merely advisory."

"It's bound to have a strong influence."

"We like to think it does." Rhonda smiled.

"Did the board recommend Butch?"

"The personnel manager selected three finalists, and we talked to all of them."

Was it my imagination, or was getting information out of her like pulling teeth? I had asked her a yes-or-no question. Was she dodging it?

I didn't repeat my question. I just tried to look expectant, as if Rhonda was going to give me an answer.

Finally she spoke. "We ranked the three we talked to."

I kept looking expectant.

"And, yes, uh—yes, Butch was our first choice."

"And did any particular board member lead the charge, so to speak, in urging the board to back Butch?"

"Butch has excellent qualifications, Lee."

"Oh yes! I've read the article about him in the *Gazette*. He sounds ideal. I guess I was just wondering if he had any local connections."

Rhonda still looked a little wary. "I don't know of any specific connections," she said. "But I will say that Abigail Montgomery thought he was the best choice.

And Miss Vanderklomp, though she doesn't have a vote, was strongly in favor of him as well."

Rhonda and I were saying good-bye as I saw Carol Turley's car skid into a parking place at the end of the block. Carol jumped out and came toward us, stumbling along with her usual awkward gait.

The final board member, I thought. At least the library had an active, responsive board. Rhonda and I walked down to meet her.

"I can't believe this!" Carol said.

"How did you hear?" Rhonda asked.

"Betty's daughter called me. The police came to her job to tell her. I guess she thought I'd know something."

"I don't think anybody knows much yet," Rhonda said. "Lee found her."

Over to me. I gave Carol a quick report of how I'd discovered Betty.

Carol had only one question. "Is she dead?"

Rhonda and I told her we assumed that she was. "It's a very strange accident," Rhonda said.

This drew an odd, sideways glance and another question from Carol. "Were both of you here when it happened?"

"No," I said. "Betty asked me to drop by after work."

"Why?"

"I have no idea. She said she had a bookkeeping question for me, but she didn't have time to tell me what it was. But she'd gone upstairs at least ten minutes before I got here."

"How do you know?"

"Because when I came in there was a line of people waiting at the circulation desk. Some of them were griping about how long they'd been waiting. If Betty had been able to come to the desk, she would have been there. She struck me as a thoroughly reliable person."

"Yes," Carol said sadly. Her hands were shaking. "Betty was always reliable."

I went home then. Somehow I wasn't surprised that Joe wasn't there when I arrived. In fact, he'd left a message for me saying he was staying in Holland for dinner for a second straight night.

Bummer.

This time I succumbed to the desire to curl up in a ball and feel sorry for myself. Not that I literally curled up in a ball. But I did put on my oldest jeans and scramble some eggs, even if I had to eat them without English muffins. I found tortillas, sharp cheese, and salsa and made some little burrito-like things.

They tasted pretty good, especially with an episode of *House Hunters* on HGTV. HGTV is definitely part of my method of curling up into a ball.

I guess I had been hungry, because I felt better after I'd eaten. I was peppy enough to rekindle my interest in Butch Cassidy's background. I did this in the full knowledge that I was indulging my crush. Yes, I recognized that I had a crush on Butch Cassidy, just the way I'd once worshipped a certain TV star, and the way Tony's older sister, Marcia, now had a crush on the teen idol Marco Spear.

It was a totally stupid way for a woman in her thirties to feel, but I didn't care. I wanted to think about him, and looking up his background was one way to do it.

I turned off the television and found the article that sketched Butch's background when he was named director of the Warner Pier Public Library.

There was his education—bachelor's degree from Western Michigan and master's from the University of Michigan. There was his upbringing—Detroit area. His early job history—U.S. Army for twenty years. He got his undergraduate degree while he was in the army. Then he held library jobs in the Ann Arbor area and at the university while he was in grad school. His age was forty-one. That meant he'd been in his late thirties before he started graduate school.

It all seemed fairly complete. But maybe there was more. I Googled him.

Henry Cassidy. University of Michigan. Information science.

A few items came up, but none sounded likely. Hmmm. I decided to take advantage of being married to a U of M graduate. I found Joe's hidden password and accessed the University of Michigan alumni lists. I searched them. I searched them again. I looked back at the article from the *Warner Pier Weekly Gazette*. Yes, it said that Butch had received his MLS the previous June. I found the list of MLS recipients. I read it. I read it again.

Finally I gave up.

Wha'd'ya know. No one named Cassidy had received an MLS from the University of Michigan in June.

As far as I could figure out from the alumni lists, Butch had never received such a degree at all.

Was my crush a fraud?

Chapter 15

Why had I wanted to know this? All it had done was make me worry, and I already had more important things to stew about.

Checking on Butch's qualifications was not my business. The city's human resources director had that responsibility.

Of course, in a town the size of Warner Pier the HR director's responsibilities averaged one hour a week and were performed by the city clerk. This wasn't Detroit. Heck, this wasn't even Dowagiac. But I was sure Butch's qualifications had been checked, and his employment had been approved. It had to be all right. My research had been superficial, and all it had done was make me unhappy.

I forced myself to face the worst possible scenario. What if Butch had lied about his qualifications to get the job in Warner Pier?

So what? It was no skin off my nose. I barely knew

Butch Cassidy. I wasn't even an official member of the library board.

But Butch had simply bowled me over. I practically panted whenever he came in the room. Why? He was an attractive, virile man, true. But the world was full of attractive men. I've been married to two of them. I got so disgusted with the first one that I divorced him, and right at the moment I wasn't too happy with the second one. So surely Butch didn't make me weak at the knees just because of his macho appearance.

And I had no intention of acting on those feelings.

Except that I had already acted on them.

By helping Butch move the letter—the letter that had been under the body of Abigail Montgomery—I had committed myself to supporting and believing in him.

Why had I done that?

I belatedly faced the fact that I might be helping a murderer.

Everybody who had been at the library board meeting on Monday had had the opportunity to kill Abigail. Any of us—Rhonda, Carol, Gwen, Corny, me, and, yes, Miss Ann Vanderklomp—could have done it. Betty Blake had had the opportunity, too, but, well, even though there was no official cause of death yet, I strongly suspected that Betty was another murder victim. Which would pretty much eliminate her as a suspect.

But of all those people, Butch was the one I'd helped to deceive the detectives. And now I discovered that he might be falsifying his credentials. But the Warner Pier city clerk was an intelligent person. She would have made a complete check of his résumé. There must have been some logical explanation for the discrepancies in his background, or she would have warned off the library board.

Still, it had been extremely foolish to lie for a man I barely knew.

Should I make an immediate confession to Hogan and Larry Underwood?

There was little point, since they had already figured it out. Neither of them had really bought my story about finding the letter in my purse.

What was wrong with me? I didn't understand my own motives. Granted, the guy was magnetic. But why would I protect him? I was sophisticated enough to know that a physical attraction was not worth acting stupid about.

And what about Joe? Here I was terribly worried about our marriage because he was seeing a girl he'd dated nearly twenty years earlier. And at the same time I was getting involved— emotionally—with another man.

Not that I was going to do anything about it. But the fact that I kept telling myself that—well, it indicated that the idea was somewhere back in the recesses of my mind.

If I were a Catholic I'd be headed for the confessional.

I closed out the computer. My thoughts on all this were extremely confused.

I had to force myself to think logically. I got up resolutely and carried my dishes into the kitchen.

And through the kitchen window I saw the headlights of a car pulling into the drive.

Joe. It must be Joe. If only I could get him to talk to me tonight. We'd hardly spoken for several days, and I desperately needed to talk to him, to communicate with him.

I went to the back door and waited for him to come up to the porch. The driver of the car was nearly there before I realized it wasn't Joe at all.

I swung the door open. "Hi, Hogan," I said. "Come on in. I was just thinking about making coffee."

"Have you got a sandwich? I never did get dinner."

"I'll fix you some of Abigail Montgomery's eggs."

"Abigail's? Nettie told me you two had cleared out her refrigerator. Eating a murder victim's eggs seems a bit kinky, but I'm so hungry I'll do it."

I made coffee and got bacon and eggs ready, and gave Hogan toast rather than tortillas. We talked about nothing while he ate. Only one touchy question came up.

"Where's Joe?" Hogan asked.

"He stayed in Holland for dinner."

"I thought this was a day he spent at the boat shop."

"It usually is."

I didn't make any other explanation. Hogan gave me a shrewd look, but he didn't demand one.

With his plate empty, he pulled out his notebook. "Okay, Lee, I'd like to have a preliminary statement about Betty Blake."

"Sure. Plus I've been trying to follow Larry Underwood's instructions and understand the personal dynamics of the library board."

"Forget Larry's instructions. From now on you stay out of the whole deal."

"Sure. But do you want to know what I found out so far?"

Hogan sighed deeply. "I guess so. You do seem to catch on to things sometimes."

I took about twenty minutes to go over the visits I'd had with the members of the library board and with Betty Blake. Hogan didn't take notes until I got to Betty.

"So," he said, "Betty called and said she wanted to talk to you about some bookkeeping problem. But she didn't give you a hint as to what it was."

"No. I don't know if it was something like—oh, which account some payment should come from. Or about how to classify income from memorial gifts. I doubt it was anything serious, because Betty's function was simply to keep records. She didn't do any complicated accounting, and Butch would do the budgeting. Or Catherine Smith would have, when she was library director. Carol Turley is secretary-treasurer, but she doesn't handle day-to-day bookkeeping."

Hogan frowned and drank coffee, then changed topics. "If Betty had been doing bookkeeping chores for several years, it seems odd that she'd have a record-keeping problem now."

"I agree. But it may have been a gift of a specific type she hadn't run into before. Something new is always coming up in every field."

"Okay. Now, about this afternoon."

I described what happened at the library. I arrived shortly before five o'clock. There was a line at the circulation desk, with no one staffing it. No sign of Betty I went back to Butch's office, and he immediately got up and went to take her place at the desk. Since Betty had asked me to come to the library, I thought she must be there someplace, so I walked around looking for her. I saw no one in the downstairs stacks. I went upstairs. I walked around the stacks near the front of the building and saw no one. When I moved to the back, I saw the shelf tipped over against the wall.

I stopped talking then and gave several big gulps. "Sorry," I said. "Seeing those shoes . . . I immediately knew it was Betty by the shoes."

"What was so special about them?"

"Oh . . . it's just that I'd noticed them when we met for lunch." I didn't want to explain that they were run-over, shabby shoes that testified to Betty's low-salaried job and the financial problems of her family. Saying that out loud would feel like a slap at Betty's pride. I gulped again and shut up.

"Was there anybody else upstairs?"

"I didn't see anyone."

"Did anyone pass you on the stairs?"

"Going down as I went up? No. I suppose someone could have hidden in the stacks up there and run for the stairs when I had my back turned. But I think I would have heard them or seen them."

I stopped for a moment, then looked closely at Hogan. "Hogan, I've been assuming that someone killed Betty. Am I right?"

"Of course, we don't . . ."

"Oh, I know! You always give out that stuff about not having an official cause of death! But are you working on the assumption that someone helped that accident happen? That someone killed her?"

"Yes, I am, Lee. Betty was the person who found Abigail Montgomery, and we're feeling real strongly that Abigail was killed by a blow to the back of the head. It's too much of a coincidence for Betty to die in a freak accident just two days later."

"So you think someone had been up there with her."

Hogan doodled an unhappy face in his notebook before he replied. "Well, there's a complication."

"What do you mean?"

"Your pal Tony Jr. I went by to talk to him before I came over here."

"And?"

"Tony was kinda miffed about having to take his

younger sister to the library for the kid's movie. He thought that was for little kids. But at the same time he, well, he sorta wanted to see the movie himself."

"I understand. Once upon a time I was thirteen myself."

"Yeah. You want to be grown up, but you want to be a kid, too. The result was that Tony found himself a seat on the stairway. From there he could look at the movie but pretend he wasn't watching it."

I chuckled.

"So Tony sat there at least for the second half of the movie. Without moving. And he swears that Betty Blake was the only person who passed him going up those stairs during that time. And nobody at all came down."

The first thing that flashed through my mind was that I'd never make a detective. I had felt sure someone killed Betty, but I'd failed to wonder who had the opportunity. I somehow assumed someone had slipped upstairs, done the dark deed, then slipped silently downstairs and out of the library.

But that isn't the way the Warner Pier Public Library works. It's just too small. The person at the desk can see almost everywhere all the time. And those stairs were the only way to get to the second story. Or were they?

"Is there a fire escape?" I asked.

"There are the back stairs."

"Then the killer must have left that way."

"Those stairs go down right by the director's office. And Butch Cassidy says he didn't see anybody. Or hear anybody. They're noisy wooden steps."

"Was Butch in the office all the time?"

"Until you called him and he took over the desk."

Hogan still looked skeptical, and I spoke sharply.

"Hogan, either someone got out by the back stairs, or Butch or I killed Betty. Take your pick."

"No, you didn't kill her," he said calmly. "We're pretty sure she was dead before you went upstairs."

Was he kidding me? No medical examiner could tell the exact minute when someone had been killed, not within a half hour or so. I looked at him narrowly.

"Plus, Tony alibis you," he said. "He says you weren't up there even five minutes."

He didn't say anything about Butch.

He left after that. But as he opened the back door, he frowned. "I don't like your being here alone," he said.

I tried to sound casual. "Oh, Joe will be along." I sure didn't want to admit I had no idea when Joe would get home. But I hated hearing the sound of Hogan's car moving away from the house.

It seemed terribly silent in our semi-rural house in our semi-rural neighborhood. I started putting dishes in the dishwasher with a tremendous clatter. I clanked and crashed and slammed pans and plates. It's a wonder I didn't break every dish I'd used. But the noise made me feel a bit less lonely.

I jumped when the phone rang.

"Mrs. Woodyard?" The caller was a woman. I didn't recognize her nasally voice.

"Yes?" Who was this? Was she selling something?

"I'm so sorry to call you so late," the voice whined. "This is Madelyn Jones."

"Jones?"

"You don't know me, but I'm—I was—a close friend of Betty Blake's."

"Oh?" Why would a friend of Betty's be calling me?

"It's her daughter. Alice Ann. She's really upset."

"I'm sure she is."

"Anyway, she'd like to talk to you."

"To me? Why?"

The whiny voice somehow became even whinier. "You were one of the last people to see her mother alive. She had some questions."

"But my meeting with Betty was just to discuss library matters. I know nothing about Betty's death."

"It would be such a help to Alice Ann."

"I really don't see—"

"Oh, Mrs. Woodyard, Alice Ann is just frantic! I think you could help us calm her right down."

I sighed deeply. How could I refuse? "Where is she?"

"At the house. Betty's house." The woman—Mrs. Jones?—gave me the address, and I said I'd come over. Before she hung up she apologized again for calling so late.

Because of the ridiculously high property values in Warner Pier, there are no shabby neighborhoods in the town. But Betty's address was in an area that was largely occupied by locals—waitresses, yardmen, sales clerks, and clerical workers; the people who do the grunt work of a resort. If we have a shabby neighborhood, that's it.

I got a jacket, wrote Joe a note, and left. I wasn't happy about the request, though I saw no way to refuse it. Being called out to comfort a person I'd never met because her mother—a person I barely knew—had died? Frankly, it stank. I did not want to go.

But I went. The temperature had dropped into the high forties by then. I started the van and switched on the heater. I kept hoping Joe would pull into the drive and offer to go with me. He didn't. I drove the two hundred feet down the sandy lane that leads from our house to Lake Shore Drive without meeting an incoming car. I turned onto Lake Shore Drive and saw no headlights coming toward me. I was alone.

Going north from our house, Lake Shore Drive follows the edge of Lake Michigan, of course. After a mile the road takes a sharp curve back to the east, and its name changes. It becomes Inland Road and leaves the lake. It follows the Warner River until the road turns left and crosses the river to link our area of Warner Pier to the rest of the town.

It's a perfectly fine road, wide and smoothly paved, with just a few tricky places. Two of these are where Lake Michigan's winter storms have washed out the bank and eaten into the shoulder of the road. The third is the sharp curve where Lake Shore Drive changes its name to Inland Road. The fourth is on the right-hand side of the road, between the two washouts, where a culvert needs repair. All four spots have guardrails, of course.

I was just about even with the first washout when lights flashed in my rearview mirror and a car pulled out onto the road behind me. I thought nothing of it. But as I drove on, the lights got brighter and brighter. The car was coming up fast.

I don't have to own the road. I dropped my speed to thirty to let the speed demon come around.

But the car didn't come around. It pulled out into the left lane, but it didn't pass me. It just came up even and drove along parallel to me.

What was going on? Was this someone I knew? I tried to see the driver, but I couldn't identify him or her. And I didn't recognize the car. It was a big SUV of some sort, a vehicle larger than my van.

I slowed down again. And I spoke aloud. "Go around, you idiot! I'm giving you the highway." But the SUV slowed, too, keeping right beside me.

The bad place on the right-hand side of Lake Shore Drive was coming up soon. I slowed again. Now I was traveling only twenty-five miles per hour. And I could see the guardrail in my headlights.

"Idiot!" I said it again just before the SUV edged over into my lane and rammed into my left-front fender.

Chocolate Chat

The consumption of chocolate may be linked to winning Nobel Prizes.

A cardiologist (apparently with too much time on his hands) studied the correlations of average national consumption of chocolate and the number of people from that nation who have been awarded Nobel Prizes.

The study was done by Franz Messerli, who is originally from Switzerland and more recently worked at St. Luike's–Roosevelt Hospital in New York. He wrote an article about it for the *New England Journal of Medicine*.

As a Swiss, Messerli noticed that his home country led in two important categories. First, the Swiss have a higher number of Nobel Prize winners than any other nation on a per-capita basis. Second, the Swiss have the world's highest average consumption of chocolate.

The comparison is obvious, Messerli said—and it's hard to say anything at all with your tongue firmly in your cheek. Eating chocolate plainly leads to winning Nobel Prizes.

Good news for young scientists. And old ones.

Chapter 16

I couldn't allow the SUV to push me into the ditch without a fight.

When I realized the thing was coming over I took evasive action, or at least I tried. I hit the brakes and I steered left into the oncoming SUV. That may have been stupid, but the steep drop on my right seemed more dangerous than a collision.

I bounced off the other vehicle, and my air bag in flated and deflated. But I managed to stay on the road. I didn't go through the guardrail, and I didn't go down into the gully. In fact, I got past the gully, which I had thought was the most dangerous spot on that stretch of road.

But that was a temporary respite. The SUV came over again, and this time I did bounce off the guardrail on my right. The SUV shot by, and the van and I did a pirouette, turning halfway around. Suddenly I was sideways across the road. And I was still moving, but this time I was going backward in slow motion.

I tried to turn the van onto the road, but it didn't work. I skidded off the road on the lake side and went down a thirty- or forty-foot bluff. A steep bluff. The nose of the van went up; the back went down. The van teetered, and for a brief, terrifying moment I thought it was going to do a backward somersault. Then the van paused in midair, fell forward, and landed on all four tires with a huge jolt. I felt as if I'd been riding a giant pancake, and I'd been slammed onto a griddle.

My ride wasn't over. Slowly, the van began to slip backward, toward the lake. I could hear bushes squeaking against the car and the cracks of what must have been small trees breaking as the van snapped them off. Then I whammed into some barrier that ended my descent.

The van and I had stopped, and I was still conscious.

The van was still conscious, too; the motor was running. I automatically slid the gearshift into park and turned off the ignition.

And that's when I got mad. I shook my fist and yelled, "I'll get you for this!"

Then I pounded the steering wheel angrily. And I growled like a bear. An angry mama bear. "The female is the most vicious of the species! I'm gonna get you for this!"

But after all that roaring—and I didn't know whom I was roaring at—I was still stuck in that van, halfway down an incline that was almost a cliff.

Could I get out of the van? Was the van going to catch fire? And, most important, was the SUV that had caused all this still up there on the road? Was its driver waiting to attack again if I got out of the van? In spite of my defiant roars, I wasn't in a very strong position to protect myself at that moment.

And in less than one minute my headlights were going to turn off, so I'd better do something about my position fast.

I popped open the glove box and felt for my flashlight. I had just picked it up when I heard a motor rev loudly, and on the road above me a vehicle dug out, going north on Lake Shore Drive.

Was it the SUV? Had my attacker fled? Why? I certainly wasn't doing anything to threaten him. Roaring might make me feel brave, but it didn't harm my attacker.

Then I heard another vehicle coming, this time from the north. The SUV must have seen that car coming and fled as a result, I decided. Maybe this new car would see me and stop to help.

And at that moment my headlights went off.

Well, that ripped it. The oncoming vehicle might be carrying a carload of rescue workers, but they weren't going to be able to see me. I was down the bluff, out of sight of the road.

I fumbled around for my headlights, cursing modern auto design. I could remember cars of my childhood. My dad would push a knob in and out, and it turned the lights off and on. Real simple. But in this van I had to twist a little gadget on the turn signal. In the dark it was impossible to see the tiny icons that told me that I was turning the knob the right way. I was still too rattled to get the flashlight on.

I gave the knob an angry twist, and miraculously the headlights went on. I was even able to flash them. I didn't make an SOS signal but I did flash them in some way. Up on the road, however, the car went on past without stopping.

I sighed. I was going to have to get myself out of this mess. I was going to have to open my door and step out onto a steep hillside without being able to see exactly where I was stepping. I didn't know how securely the van was jammed in place; at any moment it could tip over onto its side. Then it might complete its trip into the lake, taking me with it.

Not that the lake itself was much danger—right along the shore the water was likely to be shallow and have a rocky bottom. But if I slid down into it in the van, well, I could land upside down and backward and not be able to get out.

It would be risky to try to get out of the van while it was stuck halfway down the bluff. But staying where I was could be even riskier. I had to try it.

I opened the door about a foot, but that made the van rock from side to side. If it went over . . . I didn't want to think about what could happen. I turned the ignition on again—I'd left the keys in it—and I lowered the window. But that was no help.

Just as I gave another growl of frustration, a light flashed into my eyes. And I heard a voice.

"Hey! Is anybody in there?"

So help me, it was Joe.

Why not? He lived in the neighborhood.

That's when I started crying. But I swear they were tears of fury.

The next half hour is a rather confusing memory. First there was a lot of yelling, none of it very sensible.

"Joe!"

"Lee?"

"Yes! I can't get out!"

"Are you hurt?"

"No, but I'm afraid the van will roll over if I move around!"

"I'll go back up on the road and call 9-1-1! We'll get a wrecker! Don't move!"

Cell phone reception is iffy along the lakeshore. I

hoped Joe wouldn't have to find a landline to call for emergency help.

Apparently he didn't, because it was only a few minutes until Joe—still in his lawyer suit—came skidding down the bluff, waving his own flashlight around. I could see him in my headlights as he came, clinging to trees and digging his feet into the sandy soil until he reached the van. He came up beside my open window. When he spoke to me, his voice actually sounded calm.

"I think you could get out, but there's no footing except this sand. You might slip on down into the lake, and that could be bad. You'd better stay where you are until some equipment gets here."

What he wasn't saying out loud was that I could turn the van over and crush both of us. I agreed to stay where I was. "You need to back away, Joe."

"No." He took my hand.

I admit that clutching his hand was wonderful. "Do you need to go up to the road to wave the wrecker down?" I asked.

"I think I can stay here. Just don't jump around."

"Somebody pushed me off the road, and when I find out who it was, I'm going to beat them to death with a tire iron. Do you have a tissue?"

Luckily, he did. I blew my nose, and we stayed there, holding hands, until people came. Lots of people. Hogan. Jerry Cherry. The Michigan State Police. A wrecker driver. It seemed to take all of them to get me out of the van.

But they got me out. The wrecker stabilized the van with some sort of magic equipment, and I was able to climb out without turning the vehicle over. Joe and some other guys held me and kept me from sliding down into the lake; then they hauled me to the top of the bluff. Standing on the road with a firm surface under my feet felt wonderful. But I was still mad.

An ambulance came, and Joe and Hogan insisted that I ride in it to the hospital in Holland. I finally agreed, but I instructed Hogan to call Betty Blake's house and tell Betty's daughter that I couldn't come to talk to her. He frowned, but he agreed to do it.

Aunt Nettie met us at the hospital. The ER doctor declared me not only all in one piece, but darn lucky. I had no broken bones. He sent me home, warning me that I was going to be sore in every muscle, and giving me pain pills.

"I don't want pills," I said. "I'm too hyped up."

"When you come off the adrenaline high," he said, "you're going to hurt all over."

When we got home—Aunt Nettie drove us—Joe made me swallow one of those pills, then take a really hot shower. By the time I staggered to bed I was feeling no pain in either the physical or mental sense. I was barely coherent. I seem to remember talking, but I have no idea what I said. I just remember Joe lying down beside me and putting his arms around me. I tried to tell him something about Meg, but it all became jumbled in my mind with Butch Cassidy and my anger at the person in the SUV. Heaven knows what I said.

I woke up about noon, and as predicted, I hurt all over. Joe offered me another pill, but I declined.

"I've got to know what's going on," I said. "Because I've got to go kill that person who was driving the SUV. Did anybody call Betty Blake's daughter to tell her I couldn't come over?"

"Alice Ann Blake didn't want to see you, Lee."

"Then why did that woman—Madelyn? Why did she call and ask me to come?"

"Think about it."

I thought. "Oh! She wanted me to drive down Lake Shore Drive so she could shove me off."

"You got it. The phantom accident causer strikes."

"Somebody tried to kill me?"

"Right." Joe kissed me on the top of the head. "Which is why you're going to be really cautious until Hogan gets all this figured out."

"I don't want a babysitter, Joe."

"Tough. You're going to have one, at least for a while."

I sat up, and the effort caused groans. "If somebody did this to me on purpose, I'm definitely going to hurt them."

Joe didn't argue. He changed the subject. "What do you want to eat?"

"I guess I am hungry. But you'll have to go to the store. I haven't shopped in a week."

Joe laughed. "The ladies from the shop sent over enough food for an army. Do you want ham or roast beef? Slaw or three-bean salad? Chocolate cake or apple pie? Or practically anything else you can think of."

"Good heavens! You'd think I died."

"Yeah." I could see Joe gulp and blink. He looked away.

I was alive. I was glad I was alive, and Joe seemed to be glad I was alive. He gave me an enormous but gentle hug, and I hugged him back.

"Now listen, Lee," he said, "there's an important thing I have to tell you."

As if on cue, there was a knock at the back door. Then I could hear the door open, and Joe's mother, Mercy Woodyard Herrera, called out. "Hi, you two! I know you're here."

Joe laughed.

I looked at him. "And that important thing is?"

"It's that we have too many relatives." Then he called out. "Come on back to the bedroom, Mom. Lee just woke up."

Mercy had brought food, too—roast beef sandwiches, like the ones Betty and I had eaten the day before. I staggered into the dining room, with an old robe over my pajamas, and the three of us ate them. Then the phone began to ring. And Lindy Herrera came by, bringing more food. Just as she left, Maggie McNutt arrived. All afternoon I didn't have time to think about Betty Blake or Abigail Montgomery or what had happened to them or about whoever had shoved me, van and all, off the road. I stayed mad, but I was so busy with friends and family, I gave up thoughts of immediate revenge.

All this attention seemed pretty silly in a way, but I knew it was really my friends and relations telling me they loved me. So I appreciated it and reminded myself that the day would come when some crisis hit their lives, and then I'd take food and love to each of them.

About five o'clock a large sedan pulled into our lane, and Timothy Hart got out. He wasn't carrying a covered dish. No, Tim had an enormous florist's box. And his nephew, Hart VanHorn, got out of the car as well.

"Joe," I said. "Hold the fort while I put on some clothes. I'm not greeting Tim and Hart in this tacky old robe."

"You've greeted everybody else all afternoon in that tacky old robe."

"Those were people I love. I don't love Hart and Tim."

He laughed. "That's nice to hear."

"I like them. But I don't love them."

I dashed for the bedroom—or at least I walked as fast as my sore muscles would allow. I managed to pull on some brown slacks and a cream-colored sweater without moaning. Then I painted my eye-lashes and mouth for confidence. When your natural coloring is as pale as mine, it's hard to greet anybody but your best friends and your closest relatives without makeup. I might as well leave my eyes and mouth in the bedroom.

Uncle Tim and Hart came in the front door, which proved that they weren't among our closest friends. Both were dressed in slacks and blazers, and I could see a suit bag hanging in the backseat of Hart's car. They must have been on their way to Grand Rapids, where Abigail's ashes were to be buried.

Tim gave me the florist's box, which contained two dozen snazzy red roses with a personal card. I kissed Tim on the cheek and found a vase.

Luckily, Lindy had brought a commercial-sized thermos of coffee, so I was able to offer some, accompanied by TenHuis chocolates. I managed to limp into the kitchen and get out a plate of cranberry orange cinnamon truffles ("a white chocolate filling flavored with cranberry and orange, enrobed in dark chocolate and dusted with cinnamon") and French vanilla truffles ("a classic vanilla-flavored milk chocolate center covered in milk chocolate and embellished with crumbled white chocolate"). Joe served the coffee.

Our conversation was solemn, as befit the situation, but I did appreciate their coming by. And not bringing more food.

Joe and Hart knew each other in law school, so they caught up on attorney gossip, and Tim and I chatted about the neighborhood. After twenty minutes Hart checked his wristwatch, and I thought their visit was nearly over.

Then Tim reached into his pocket. "Here, Lee. I want you to keep this for the moment."

"What is it, Tim?"

"It's that key." He held out the little brass key.

"Is this the one from Abigail's lettuce? Why do you want me to have it?"

Tim smoothed his white mustache. "I can't help but feel that the key has some meaning, something to do with Abigail's death."

"Why?"

"She had other extra keys. House keys, car keys, safety-deposit box keys. They were in her desk. That was the only key she had hidden away."

"But why do you want me to have it?"

"Hart wants me to go to Grand Rapids with him for a couple of weeks. I just think someone here on the spot should keep it."

"Should you give it to Hogan?"

Tim shook his head. "It may not have anything to do with Abigail's death. But if it does, you should be close enough to the situation to figure it out and give it to Hogan if he needs it."

I took the key and put it on the mantelpiece, beside the roses, and Joe and I said good-bye to Tim and Hart.

We were beginning to think about warming up some more of that food when another car, a gray compact, came up the lane. Neither of us recognized it. Again, it parked in front of the house, so we knew it wasn't a close friend or relative.

But I was still astonished when Carol Turley and her husband, Brian, got out.

I muttered. "Now what?"

It belatedly occurred to me that I'd discussed Abigail Montgomery with every member of the library board except one.

Carol Turley. Why had I ignored her?

Chapter 17

While Carol and Brian were walking up to our front door I analyzed that question further. And the answer was embarrassing.

I hadn't given Carol and her relations with Abigail any attention because Carol seemed so unimportant. She was a member of several community organizations, true, and she guarded the finances of each of them. But she didn't really seem to matter to me or to Warner Pier.

In fact, her whiny attitude and dud personality made her easy to ignore. It wasn't fun to think about her, so I didn't. No one seemed to.

This was not nice, I told myself. Carol was a hard-working person. She deserved more credit and attention. If she got some appreciation, maybe she wouldn't be so whiny. I set out to be a welcoming and appreciative hostess, even if I hurt in every muscle and wished Carol and Brian hadn't come.

True to small-town life, Carol had brought something. But it wasn't food. She held her red leather folder, of course, but she also had a book, which she presented to me. I read the title. *Playing the Game of Life* by Brian Turley. I checked the title page. Self-published. Hmmm.

"Of course, I'm prejudiced, but I think Brian did a really good job," she said. "I thought if you were in bed for a few days . . ."

"I hope to go back to work tomorrow," I said. "But thanks for the book. I'll look at it soon." I'll look at it on the way to the trash, I thought. It seemed to be the kind of pop philosophy that I find more annoying than inspiring. But I reminded myself that it was nice of Carol to think of me at all.

I put the book on the mantelpiece, next to the flowers Tim had brought. As I did so, I saw the key from the hiding place in Abigail's lettuce. I scooped it up and put it in the pocket of my slacks.

I heard Carol give a little gasp. I looked at her in surprise. "Is something wrong?"

"No, not at all! It's just that those are such lovely flowers! Did Joe send them to you?"

"Oh no. They're from a neighbor. Joe knows I'd scalp him if he spent the family budget on flowers."

Carol gave a sad little smile. "It's hard to get them to understand budgeting, isn't it?"

"I see you handle the family finances, too."

"If you're a bookkeeper, you sort of get stuck with it."

"What about your business finances?"

Carol's eyes became slits. "What do you mean?"

"Don't you and your husband operate a camp?"

"Oh! Yes. Camp Upright. Of course, Brian runs it. But, yes, I do the bookkeeping."

I realized Joe was bringing in more coffee, and Brian was behind him, carrying napkins. He was a handsome, athletic-looking guy, maybe around thirty-five, with dark, wavy hair and a grin that showed lots of teeth. He was nearly as good-looking as the picture on the back of his book.

As they came into the living room Brian was talking. "Up to a hundred campers," he said.

I realized that Joe was doing his I-can-talk-to-anybody act. He wasn't all that interested in camps, but he was feeding questions to Brian. "What age group are the kids?"

"We have different sessions for the different age groups," Brian said. "But most of them are middle-schoolers."

Luckily, there were truffles left on the coffee table from Tim and Hart's visit. I handed them around, Joe served coffee, and we settled in for another formal call, one I hoped wouldn't last too long.

I realized pretty quickly, however, that any time at all with Brian was going to be too long for me. He was one of these people who are hipped on their own subject, so we heard all about Camp Upright and nothing else. He told us how lucky they were that Carol had inherited the property where it was located. Then he described its physical plant—first as it was at the present, and next what he wished it were, with various updates. Then he went on to the camp program, which stressed athletics as a pathway to mental health and morality.

Carol didn't say much. Her role seemed to be looking at Brian adoringly. She reminded me of the wife of a political candidate, looking enthralled while her husband gave a stump speech she'd already heard at least a hundred times.

Brian wasn't boring. I wasn't in the mood for his spiel, but he was handsome and lively. He'd be a great speaker for a civic club, and I could see that he might be able to inspire young athletes. Male athletes, that is. I asked about programs for girls and got a brief lecture on "physical limitations."

When he went into a really heartfelt story about a track star who dedicated his life to sportsmanship—under Brian's tutelage, of course—I turned to Carol and spoke quietly, starting a second conversation.

"What was your take on Abigail?"

Carol jumped. Then she pulled her attention from Brian to me and said, "My take?"

"Yes. What did you think of her?"

"She was a very nice person."

How was that for a bland answer? I decided to push a little harder. "What did you feel was her major interest on the library board?"

"Major interest?"

"You know. Did she want to expand the collections? Or expand the usage? Or offer more programs?" I shrugged. "Or something else?"

"All of those things, I guess. She didn't argue with Mrs. Smith much. None of us did."

"Her brother told me she worked for an accounting firm during her working career. Did she give you trouble over the books?"

"No! Why should she?"

"No reason, Carol. It's just that people who have worked in accounting have their favorite ways of doing things. Sometimes we like to inflict them on our fellow bookkeepers."

Carol sniffed. "I've always tried to use standard accounting practices for the few items I handle. The library staff and the city treasurer do nearly everything, of course. Abigail never made any comment."

That seemed to cover that subject. I sipped my coffee and prepared to listen to Brian's monologue.

But Carol blurted out a question. "They're saying someone deliberately tried to push you off the road, Lee."

"That's about the size of it."

"But who would do such a thing?"

"I have no idea. I didn't recognize the vehicle the person was driving. And I didn't see who was driving it. But I sure want to find out."

"I'm so glad you weren't badly hurt." The words were spoken woodenly.

Neither of us seemed to have any more conversation, so we both turned back to Brian. He was telling Joe about how the camp was supported financially.

"We have to get scholarships for a lot of the kids," he said. "I go to the civic clubs and fraternal organizations, but they're not as strong as they used to be. Of course, some people make in-kind gifts."

"You mean like food? Or equipment?"

"Right. The food supplier gives us a good rate on milk, for example. And we have a little give-a-boat program. A couple of years ago, when there were so many economic setbacks, people couldn't afford to keep up their boats, and they couldn't sell them, so several people just gave them to us. It's allowed us to have a good boating program. Plus—"

That was the moment when I did a lousy job of hiding a yawn. Carol apparently noticed, and she immediately jumped up. "Brian! We'd better go. Lee needs to rest."

"But, Carol, I was just telling Joe—"

"You can tell him another time." She started toward the door.

Brian almost pouted. "Okay, Carol." He sounded quite annoyed as he spoke to Joe. "That program has been very effective in gaining donations from—"

"Brian!" I was surprised at how sharp Carol's voice became. Brian rolled his eyes like a twelve-year-old and followed her.

Joe and I walked them to the door, but we didn't part with that standard remark about hoping we saw them again soon. We just said, "Thanks for coming."

But after they drove off, Joe said something that struck me as significant. "Why on earth did they come anyway?"

"I guess Carol is one of those people who visit the sick," I said. "Whether they want to be visited or not."

"We need to talk, but let's eat dinner before somebody else shows up," Joe said. "A couple of TenHuis bonbons go only so far in fighting hunger."

"Truffles, Joe. Those were truffles."

We headed for the kitchen, made our selections from the refrigerator, warmed stuff up in the microwave, and loaded our plates. I was really tired again, and I was hoping that calling hours were over, but before we could sit down Aunt Nettie and Hogan came by.

Joe threw open the back door. "You'll have to wait on yourselves, but come in and eat dinner."

They did. We had reached the chocolate-cake stage when Hogan admitted why he had come. "I need a statement from you, Lee. After all, someone tried to kill you."

I laid down my fork. "And I'm going to make whoever did that sorry."

"I understand how you feel. But let's start with a statement." Aunt Nettie and Joe cleared the table, and Hogan began to question me.

Hogan didn't ask much about the commotion when the SUV hit me and I hit the railing and went down the bluff backward. No, he wanted to know about the woman who had called me. What did she sound like? Was her voice familiar? Did she use any unusual expressions or words?

My answer to most of these questions was, "No." I hadn't recognized her voice. It hadn't reminded me of anyone.

"Unless it was Tony Herrera," I said.

"Tony?" Hogan was incredulous.

"A couple of weeks ago Tony was imitating Miss Ann Vanderklomp. As a joke. He held his nose when he talked—you know, so he would sound really nasal, the way Miss Vanderklomp does. This person who called— the one who gave her name as Madelyn Jones—her voice had that nasal tone."

I leaned over to emphasize what I was saying. "Hogan, I'm not saying that the woman on the phone could have been Miss Vanderklomp. I'm just saying she had a nasal tone like Miss Vanderklomp does. And I'm afraid that means she was imitating her. So I think we can conclude that the gal on the phone—the mysterious Madelyn—definitely doesn't sound like Miss Vanderklomp."

"Since the voice was disguised . . . could it have been a man on the phone?"

I closed my eyes and tried to remember. "Maybe."

He sipped his coffee, and we both thought about that possibility. "Well, using a nasal voice may tell us something important," Hogan said.

"What's that?"

"The caller knows Miss Vanderklomp."

"Not necessarily. Miss Vanderklomp isn't the only

person with a nasal voice. Besides, that wouldn't narrow it down much. Don't most people in Warner Pier know Miss Vanderklomp?"

"People of a certain age do. But the person who called you also knows Betty Blake's family. Alice Ann really is the name of Betty's daughter, for example. Your caller knew that."

"In a town this size, a lot of people know Betty's family."

"Did you know Betty's family? Did you know Miss Vanderklomp?"

"Well, I just met Miss Vanderklomp last week. But of course I'd heard of her before."

Hogan kept looking at me expectantly.

"I didn't know the names of Betty's children," I said. "I didn't even know Betty's name until the night of the library board meeting. I'd seen her at the library, but our conversation was, 'I'd like to check out this book,' from me, and, 'It's due in two weeks,' from her. She had a nameplate, but I'd barely glanced at it."

"But it's strongly likely that the person who called knew both Betty Blake and Miss Vanderklomp. So the caller is probably someone local."

I wasn't convinced that this was valuable information, though Hogan seemed to feel that he was accomplishing something. But when I bluntly asked him if he felt he was getting close to figuring out who killed Abigail Montgomery, he evaded the question.

Then he looked at me closely. "Lee, I hope you're not serious about killing the person who drove the SUV."

"Not unless he or she tries to kill me again. I definitely would fight for my life."

"Good girl! You'd be perfectly justified. But I don't want you seeking that person out."

"I know. If I did, you might have to arrest me." I

leaned closer to Hogan. "You and your pal Larry Underwood thought I was in a good position to learn things about the library board members."

"That hasn't worked out very well. I think you ought to stay away from the library board crowd."

I didn't reply, so Hogan spoke again. "Lee? Can we shake on that?"

"No."

"Listen, Lee. Your aunt and I love you, you know. We don't want anything to happen to you."

"I appreciate that, Hogan, and believe me, I don't want anything to happen to me either. I can't promise that I will ignore anything that falls in front of me, but I won't take any silly risks either. But I can't just say I'll avoid the library crowd."

I admit that avoiding Butch Cassidy didn't appeal to me.

He and Aunt Nettie left, and I took another hot shower. The hot water sluicing over my sore muscles did seem to help them feel less sore.

It also encouraged thought. I analyzed my situation.

First, I had been among the first people on the scenes of two murders.

Second, someone had tried to kill me.

Third, the killer must believe I was a threat to him or her. I didn't see how I could be—I had no evidence I hadn't given the investigators—but the bad guy or gal evidently thought I knew more than I really did.

What could I do about it? I couldn't sit at home, being guarded by my husband for the rest of my life.

And speaking of my husband, were my problems with that husband doing better?

Twenty-four hours earlier Joe had been staying late in Holland. I had had no idea where he was, but I had suspected he was seeing Meg Corbett. I hadn't specifically feared that they were getting cozy in a motel; I was more fearful of Meg's emotional appeal to Joe than of her physical attraction.

Let's face it: Meg wasn't the kind of woman to hand out sexual favors without expecting to get something out of it. I wasn't sure Joe had anything to give her that she would be interested in trading for. But she'd been Joe's first serious girlfriend. She still attracted him the same way she had been when he was sixteen. That was what scared me. It wasn't that Meg wanted Joe; it was that Joe had never gotten over wanting Meg.

But for the past twenty-four hours Joe seemed to have lost all interest in her. He had saved my life by finding me in my wrecked van. He had held my hand until the wrecker, police, and ambulance came. He had insisted I see a doctor. He had gone to the hospital with me. He had tenderly put me to bed and given me a pain pill. He had waited on me hand and foot all day long. He had served visitors coffee. He had fixed my dinner—well, he hadn't had to cook it, but he made sure I ate. He had been nice to my callers—even Brian and Carol Turley.

I had absolutely no complaints about Joe's actions or behavior. He had been the perfect husband.

Gosh! I guess he loved me. He'd certainly acted as if he did.

When I turned off the shower I felt warm all over, and it wasn't just from the scalding hot water. Joe's concern and love were so wonderful that I didn't feel at all frightened of the mysterious person who had shoved me off the road and down the bluff. It was as if I were surrounded by a wall of love that simply wouldn't let anything harm me. And "anything" included Meg. I didn't understand just what was going on there, but I was sure it was something innocent. Because I was obviously the one Joe cared about, big-time. We were forever.

When I turned off the exhaust fan and opened the bathroom door I could hear Joe in the living room, talking.

That's typical of our house, built in 1904. There are no secrets in it. Whatever you say upstairs can be heard downstairs. Whatever is said in the kitchen is audible in the bedroom. And conversation in the living room broadcasts everywhere under the roof.

"I'll be in touch tomorrow." That was all Joe said.

When I went into the bedroom, he was coming in from the living room. "Are you out of the bathroom?" he asked.

"Yep. It's all yours. Who called?"

"One of the women from the shop. I confess that I didn't get her name."

I put my arms around him. "You've been a wonderful husband today—as usual! You've made me feel petted and cared for. And I do appreciate it. Thank you."

Joe returned my embrace and murmured in my ear. "It's easy to pet you, Lee. Believe me. When I think . . . Well, I don't want anything to happen to you." He backed away slightly and looked at me. "Are you getting in bed already?"

"I might read for a few minutes."

"You ought to take a pain pill again tonight. Just to make sure you sleep really well."

"I'd rather not unless I really need one."

"We never did get to talk. Maybe before you doze off." Joe emptied his pockets onto the dresser and went into the bathroom for his own shower. Meanwhile, I decided I'd better double-check to be sure all that food had been put away, and I wandered into the kitchen. I made a few adjustments—putting the squash casserole in a smaller dish and stashing half the leftover ham in the freezer.

When I had everything arranged I picked up the phone and asked it who had called recently. I did wonder who Joe had been talking to. The phone indicated no one had called the house in the past hour.

Well, Joe had been talking to someone. They must have called on his cell phone. That was an odd thing for one of the ladies from the shop to do. How would a person Joe didn't know all that well get his cell number?

I went into the bedroom and picked up Joe's phone from the dresser. I checked recent incoming calls. No one had called him either. Had he been talking to himself?

Obviously not. Plainly Joe had called someone. I checked outgoing calls.

And the name Meg Corbett popped up on the tiny screen.

I didn't bawl or pitch a fit. I needed to think about this. But I didn't want to talk about it.

I took a pain pill and got in bed.

Chapter 18

I know it would have been smarter to wait until Joe was out of the shower, then simply say, "Joe, what's going on with you and Meg?"

I think he would have explained things. And even if he had given me the worst possible answer, I would have known what was going on. Not understanding the situation was part of what was driving me crazy.

But I didn't do the smart thing. Joe and I had had one fight about Meg. I didn't want to have another. All of a sudden I hurt all over, and I was tired. I gulped that pill down and climbed in bed. I had a vague memory of Joe coming in and saying, "Lee?" I think I muttered something about taking his advice about the pain pill. I was dimly aware that he wandered around in the bedroom for a while. Then I was out.

The next morning I woke up while it was still dark. The memory of Joe's call to Meg woke with me, and I lay there and planned how to deal with it. With the energy that came from a night's sleep, I wasn't so eager to avoid a confrontation. I planned just what I was going to say. "Hey, Joe, what's going on with Meg? Last night I checked to see who had called while I was in the shower, and I figured out you'd been talking to her."

There. That was simple. It didn't include anything accusatory, like, "Why the heck did you call Meg?"

I could say my piece at the breakfast table.

Then I turned over and saw that Joe wasn't in bed. I sat up and realized the house was quiet. Joe wasn't there at all.

The silence made me feel a little panicky, so I quickly jumped up and turned on the light. To my relief, Joe had left a note on the mirror. "I've got to be at the office in Holland early today. Hogan said he'd put a patrol car in our drive, and Jerry can take you to work if you decide to go in."

At least the note was signed "Love, Joe." I didn't quite clutch the message to my bosom, but I did hang on to that phrase with emotional desperation.

I was still sore all over, but I felt much better, so I got myself ready for the office. The phone rang once, but I didn't recognize the number, so I let the machine pick it up. I was surprised to hear the voice of Miss Ann Vanderklomp.

"Mrs. Woodyard, I have no wish to bother you, but we do need to have a short discussion. May I drop by about noon? I promise not to take much of your time."

I rolled my eyes and picked up the phone. "Miss Vanderklomp? I'm sorry I didn't get to the phone before the answering machine picked up. I'll be glad to talk to you at any time. I'm planning to go to the office today. Can you come by TenHuis Chocolade?"

"That would be entirely convenient. Is noon a good time?"

"Certainly," I said. "Can you tell me what it is you wish to discus? I mean, discuss?" She had me talking like a nineteenth-century novel, one with a tongue-tied heroine.

Miss Vanderklomp gave a titter. "It is a matter of some delicacy. I'll see you at noon."

I put on the same brown slacks and cream-colored sweater I'd worn the previous evening. Next I made a pot of coffee and waved at Jerry Cherry, the patrolman stationed in our driveway. He came in for coffee and toast. Then he drove me to the office.

"I don't deserve all this personal service," I said.

"Hogan's really worried about this attack on you, Lee. He wants to make sure nothing else happens. Besides, your car is not drivable."

"I forgot that! But having a personal chauffeur seems a bit much."

"Once you're at the shop, you're on your own. Just don't go off by yourself. Okay?"

"Can I go to the post office?"

Jerry grinned. "If you look both ways before you cross the street."

It took me a while to get to the bank and the post office, of course. The detectives in books usually don't have to fool with friends, relatives, and coworkers. I had to thank everyone for the food, assure Aunt Nettie I had slept well and felt better, and answer four phone calls from friends checking on how I was doing after my terrible experience. And, no, you can't tell them to hang up and get out of your hair.

So it was ten o'clock before I started out the door with my bank deposit in one hand and the key to the PO box in the other. Yes, I looked up and down the street carefully before I stepped out the door. I didn't see anybody with a gun, a knife, or a bottle of poison, so I started up the street, and I made it to the bank before I was waylaid.

"Lee! Lee!" I immediately recognized Butch's voice. I turned to see him coming toward me at a swift walk. "You look as if you're okay! I heard the worst stories about you being in a wreck."

"I look a lot better than my van does."

"I'm sorry!"

"How's the library dealing with the latest crisis?"

"We closed yesterday, but today we're back to what passes for normal. Chief Jones is even letting us use the basement."

"Have they set the services for Betty?"

"Tuesday, I think. Two o'clock at her church. The library board members sent a ham to the house."

"Betty's going to be hard to replace." I remembered that Betty had wanted Butch's job. I wondered if he knew. I wasn't going to mention it.

Butch gave a deep sigh, as if he were steeling himself. "Listen, Lee. I told Chief Jones about that letter."

"You did? He didn't mention it to me."

"No! No! I didn't tell him about how it got in your purse. I mean, I told him about where it came from and why I was touchy about it."

"Oh."

Butch looked up at the trees. He might have explained the letter to Hogan, but I could see he wasn't going to tell me about it. "Anyway," he said, "I'm glad you're back on your feet."

We exchanged a long look. Then he turned abruptly and walked away.

Had that look been meaningful? Darned if I knew. I had that sinking feeling in my innards again.

Darn! He was sexy. And how could I be mad at Joe

for seeing an old girlfriend while I was having serious flutters over Butch Cassidy? Crazy!

But the word "seeing" was the key, I decided. Though small-town life meant that I saw Butch—at meetings or just casually at the bank, or even in restaurants—I wasn't deliberately seeking him out. I thought Joe had been seeking Meg out. Or maybe she was seeking him out.

At any rate, it was potentially a mess, and I wasn't about to get into what they call an open marriage. No. That was out.

I came out of the bank determined to think about something else, and Butch's comments had given me guidance on what. That letter. The one that had been under Abigail Montgomery's body. Why was it so important?

Did it have anything to do with my questions about Butch's qualifications? I still didn't understand why he didn't show up as a University of Michigan alum. That might not be any of my business, but I wanted to know.

So as soon as I had my bank deposit made and my mailbox emptied, I headed back to my computer. And I looked up the name that had been on the return address of the mysterious letter under Abigail's body. I typed in "Henry C. Dunlap" and "Michigan." Since Butch had apparently lived in Michigan except when he was in the army, that seemed a likely connection.

Of course, nearly all the references were to genealogical sites, but halfway down I found a newspaper story. I clicked on it. And five minutes later I closed it, heartsick.

The Henry C. Dunlap in the article had been found innocent of murder by reason of insanity.

Twenty years earlier, in a small town near Detroit, he had shot his wife and daughter dead and had wounded his twenty-two-year-old son. The son, Henry Cassidy Dunlap Jr., nicknamed Butch, had been on leave from the U.S. Army. He had testified that his father's personality had changed dramatically about three years earlier. "He and I began having trouble," he had said on the stand. "I felt that if I left home things might improve, so I enlisted in the army. Now I'm afraid I abandoned my mother and sister to a hopeless situation. I should have stayed there to protect them."

Tragic. No wonder Butch had decided to change his name. It would be no fun having busybodies like me dig up the family secrets. Feeling ashamed, I closed the file.

And the name change undoubtedly explained why Butch didn't turn up in the University of Michigan alumni listings. He'd probably changed his name about the time he graduated.

Speaking of secrets, Miss Ann Vanderklomp was due in an hour. Until then I would try to get a little work done.

Miss Vanderklomp was right on time, of course. Since this was a formal call, I met her in the shop and escorted her into my office. I had prepared a small dish of sample truffles and bonbons. She picked the dark chocolate cheesecake truffle ("creamy white chocolate center flavored with cream cheese and encased in dark chocolate"). She then declined coffee, and I said, "What can I do for you?"

Miss Vanderklomp's voice sounded more nasal than ever. "I'm afraid it will seem an odd request."

"As long as it's not chocolate-covered ants, we can handle it."

"Oh, it's nothing to do with chocolate. It's about a key."

"A key?"

"Yes. You may know that I had borrowed some space in the current library building. It was excess for library needs, and Mrs. Smith gave me permission to use it."

"Oh?"

"At any rate, there should be only one key for it, but somehow a second one was made."

I was mystified. "A second key?"

"Yes. The key is unusual." She smiled. "It's quite old. The lock was installed in my great-grandfather's day."

Of course, I knew immediately that she was talking about the key that Timothy Hart had brought me. But Tim hadn't left it with me so I could hand it over to Miss Vanderklomp. No, he had given it to me in case it turned out to be linked to his sister's death. Then I was to give it to Hogan.

I was not going to hand the key over to Miss Vanderklomp. Or tell her anything about it.

I immediately saw that keeping my resolve might not be easy. Miss Vanderklomp smiled what she probably thought was a winning smile. "I understand that you have the key. So I'd appreciate its return."

I couldn't just deny having the key. I had to face her down.

Well, I knew enough about arguing not to quibble. If you are going to say no, just say no. Don't let 'em shake you into making a lot of different arguments.

"Please give me the key," Miss Vanderklomp said.

"No," I said.

That summed up the rest of our conversation. Miss Vanderklomp cajoled, an action she obviously wasn't used to. I refused.

She stayed at least another ten minutes, giving me the reasons she should have the key. It had belonged to her grandfather. She was entitled to have it. The whole question was silly—the key was obviously hers. I was keeping it illegally. Or so she said.

I said, "No." I said it repeatedly.

Miss Vanderklomp's problem was that she had no authority to back her up. I could have, if I hadn't gotten by with "no," said I'd ask Hogan what to do. But she had no fall-back position. She demanded the key, but she didn't have a convincing reason for me to give it to her.

Miss Vanderklomp wasn't used to having her desires opposed. She always got her own way, just with the strength of her personality. But by flatly opposing her—and not discussing it—I carried the day.

I doubt I could have stood against her if I'd started citing arguments. She did have a powerful personality, and she could probably have destroyed any reason I came up with to deny her the key. But by just saying no, I was sneaky enough to battle her.

Finally she stood up and thundered at me. "I find your attitude most uncooperative, Mrs. Woodyard."

"I'm sorry you feel that way, Miss Vanderklomp, but I must do what I think is right."

"You haven't heard the last of this."

"I'll be here if you wish to discuss it further."

She turned toward the door, and stopped dead in her tracks. The whole shop was staring at her. The girl on the sales counter was facing us, and Aunt Nettie and the hairnet ladies were craning their necks to see through the door from the workshop.

I didn't laugh, but it was a struggle. I stood up, concentrating on looking dignified and hoping Miss Vanderklomp couldn't see the key outlined in my pocket. It was still where I had stuck it the previous evening when I realized Carol was eyeing it. I felt so self-conscious about it that the key might as well have been like a neon light shining through the fabric of my slacks.

I escorted Miss Vanderklomp to the front door. Then I went into the back room, and Aunt Nettie and I hooted with laughter.

"I never thought I'd see the day," she said. "You skunked her, Lee. I'm really proud of you."

I was proud of myself, too. There was only one catch in all this: I still had no idea what that darn key opened.

But at least I knew it was for an area in the Warner Pier Public Library. And I was willing to bet it was in the basement, because Miss Vanderklomp had made such a concerted effort to get in there.

And the library was open today, I realized. Butch Cassidy had told me that when I ran into him at the bank. Hogan had even declared that the basement was no longer a crime scene.

I had to get there fast.

I stopped laughing, grabbed my cell phone, and ran out the front door of the shop. I called Hogan as I walked along. Of course, since I really needed him, he didn't answer his cell phone, and the dispatcher at the police station said he wasn't there. She promised to try to get hold of him and tell him to meet me at the library.

"Immediately!" I said. "It's important."

The dispatcher sighed. "You're the third person to leave that message," she said.

I clicked off the phone and ran up the library steps. A young woman I hadn't seen before was at the circulation desk. I ran past her and went straight to Butch's office. It was locked. It was twelve forty-five. He was probably at lunch.

I ran back to the desk and pushed in front of an elderly woman checking out mystery novels. "Has Miss Ann Vanderklomp been in today?"

The young woman stared at me, openmouthed. "No. No, I haven't seen her."

"Is Butch—is Mr. Cassidy out to lunch?"

She nodded.

"Do you have his cell number?"

She shook her head.

"I desperately need to talk to him. The minute he comes back in, tell him I'm looking for something in the basement, and he needs to know about it."

I turned away, headed for the basement stairs.

"Wait a minute!" The young woman's voice was frantic. "Who are you?"

I told her my name, then toyed with the idea of giving a fuller explanation. I gave it up. Any explanation would simply take too long. I just headed for the basement.

Since the crime-scene tape was gone, I went right down—negotiating the steep steps carefully. I found a light switch at the top, and I held the handrail. The staircase still shook. I didn't want to wind up in a crumpled heap at the bottom, the way Abigail had, and that could happen even without the treatment Abigail had apparently had from a blunt instrument.

I found a second light switch at the bottom of the stairs, but when I clicked it, the bulb hanging over the stairs went off. So I quickly clicked it on again. Then I looked around for other lights. I found the hanging—swinging—bulb I'd turned on the night Abigail was killed, and I looked around until I found two more. I pulled the chains that turned them on, and wished that I'd brought the powerful flashlight from my car. Then I ground my teeth and remembered that I had no car. The van was unlikely ever to be on the road again.

I put that thought out of my mind and turned around slowly, looking the basement over. So I was there. In the place where I was sure some important clue was hidden. But what could I do about it? Where should I search? The whole area just looked—well, it looked like an old basement that's been accumulating junk for a hundred and seventy-five years.

Not that the area was particularly crowded. Anything that was likely to be needed in the new library had apparently been moved out already. The things that were still down there actually were junk, or maybe antiques. There were broken chairs, piles of dilapidated books, and a few old filing cabinets. Nearly everything had been pushed against the walls. There was nothing exciting, and nothing that could be opened by a skeleton key.

I needed to look systematically. First I circled the room, looking at all the walls, making sure there wasn't another room behind some of the stuff.

If there was, I saw no evidence of it. Three of the walls and the floor were concrete—old, cracked concrete painted white. Only the back wall, one of the two narrower walls, was wooden. It was paneled with bead board, a material used in the teens and twenties—the 1910s and 1920s. I knew because we had some of it in the kitchen and bathroom in our old house. Old bookshelves and book carts with broken wheels were pushed against it.

I was still standing in the middle of the big room, staring all around, when I heard footsteps on the wooden steps, and Butch came down. "What are you up to?" he asked.

I quickly explained, ending with, "So I feel sure Miss Vanderklomp is looking for something down here, and I'd like to find it before she does."

Butch nodded. "That confirms my feeling. In fact, I asked Hogan Jones to keep the basement door locked a day longer than he intended to so I could keep her out. But you say you've got a key?"

"Yes, and she tried to get it away from me." I took the key from my pocket and showed it to Butch. He examined it, then handed it back.

"It seems to be for a cabinet or cupboard."

"Yes, but there isn't such a thing down here."

Butch walked over to the bead-board wall. "This would be the only possibility." He gave a gasp. "You know, there's a window in that back wall—it's visible from outside. But there's no window in here."

"Come on, Butch! I refuse to think about a secret room."

"Pretty cornball, I agree. But let's look behind all this junk."

We approached the back wall. Butch started at the left end, and I started at the right. We pulled everything away from the wall. Nothing was there. Just more bead board. And lots of old furniture that scraped on the concrete floor as we moved it.

Until we met in the center of the wall. A rolling cart stood there, and when I yanked at it, it easily flew away from the wall and nearly ran over me.

"Oh gosh!" I said.

"And golly darn," Butch said. "You've found it."

I pushed the cart out of the way and looked where Butch was pointing. There, in plain view, was a keyhole. And once we'd found the lock, the outlines of the door were easy to see. It was made of bead board, just like the wall, and the ridges in the paneling had made the door invisible until we found the lock.

I pulled out the mysterious key that had been stored in Abigail's fake lettuce. "Do we dare?"

"We don't dare not to," Butch said.

"You're the library director. You open it." I handed him the key.

"It probably doesn't fit."

But it did fit. The skeleton key slipped right into the keyhole, and it turned smoothly.

"The lock's been oiled recently," Butch said. He pushed the door open.

Inside was a closet about five feet deep and running both right and left for the full width of the basement. And, sure enough, there was a window high in the center of the outside wall, a window that overlooked the alley. The closet was lined with narrow shelves—four shelves on each side of the area, each of them about a foot deep. A two-foot aisle down the middle gave access to the shelves.

And the shelves were lined with books.

Neither of us spoke. Butch reached for the nearest shelf and took down a book. We both backed out of the closet and turned so that the nearest hanging bulb cast its light on the book.

I began to laugh.

Butch spoke. "My God!" he said. "It's Nancy Drew!"

Chocolate Chat

Swedish research indicates that eating chocolate bars can help fight strokes.

As reported in the British publication the *Guardian*, Susanna Larsson of the Karolinska Institute looked at food questionnaires from nearly forty thousand men between forty-nine and seventy-five in age. She compared these to hospital records showing how many of these men had strokes.

She then compared their reported chocolate consumption with the number of strokes the group had suffered.

She discovered that men with the highest consumption of chocolate had seventeen percent fewer strokes compared with the men who ate no chocolate at all.

Flavonoids, chemicals found in chocolate, were given the credit by Larsson.

The beneficial effects of chocolate had been reported earlier, but they had largely been linked to eating dark chocolate. However, Larsson's study used milk chocolate. She said that about ninety percent of the chocolate consumed in Sweden is milk chocolate.

The research dealt only with men—but surely that means "men" in the sense of "mankind." Right?

Chapter 19

"I'll bet this is one of the Nancy Drew books Lindy gave the library," I said.

Butch looked puzzled, and I explained that one of my friends had donated her mother's childhood books for the library's collection but had never seen them on the shelf. "She was a bit hurt about it."

"We'll look the books over," Butch said.

Under one of the hanging lights, he pulled the book cart that had hidden the door, and we began to sample the books inside the closet. We each pulled about a dozen books from the shelves and piled them on the cart. Then we stood side by side and looked through our collections.

As I had suspected, there had been about twenty-five Nancy Drews on one shelf, and I brought one of them. On a different shelf was a large collection of Hardy Boys books, and I even found a group of ancient Tarzan novels. "These might be valuable to a collector," I said.

Butch's sampling included Westerns—he said he'd seen one group of about twenty Zane Grey paperbacks—plus ten-year-old paperback romances, and a graphic novel.

What fascinated me was that we didn't find any books commonly identified as "dirty," the ones on those lists of books often removed from library shelves either because of their prurient content or because of the supposedly controversial ideals they supported.

No, the books we found I would have called harmless. The quality of the writing might not be very high. But they weren't the usual books yanked off the library shelf by self-proclaimed moralists.

The Nancy Drew book I'd picked up, for example, wasn't from the 1930s, the editions I call the "sinister Chinaman" versions because of their politically incorrect language and attitudes. No, it was from the 1960s, a version that had been updated for its era.

I remembered Lindy saying that Miss Vanderklomp had once bawled her out in front of the whole school for reading a romance. It appeared that the retired English teacher was still trying to upgrade the reading taste of Warner Pier.

I repeated Lindy's story to Butch.

"That's as good an explanation as we're likely to find," he said. "I guess Miss Vanderklomp has been going through the donated books and picking out the ones she didn't think were up to, well, some standard that exists in her own mind."

We stared at our collection for a long moment, then we spoke at the same time, and we said the same thing.

"I wonder if she had to read all of these books?"

Then we both burst into gales of laughter. I pictured Miss Vanderklomp carefully picking out objectionable books, then having to read each of them to make sure it wasn't worthy of the shelves of the Warner Pier Public Library. The idea was hilarious.

The two of us stood there laughing until I began to feel weak. I leaned on the book cart, then, without knowing exactly how it happened, I found I was leaning against Butch. And he was leaning in my direction.

I looked up at him. Oh no, I thought. He's going to kiss me.

We looked into each other's eyes for a long moment. Then we both looked away.

And from above us, I heard a voice.

"What's so funny?"

I jumped. Butch jumped. The book cart rolled away. And I whirled toward the sound.

Because it was Joe's voice. I had nearly kissed the man I'd been lusting after, and my husband had witnessed the whole episode.

Golly!

Fifteen years earlier, when I was in my mid-teens, my parents realized they had a great big, tall, awkward daughter on their hands. They couldn't do anything to make me short or dainty, but they had the idea that some sort of charm-school classes would help me be less awkward. So that was the present they gave me for my sixteenth Christmas. And I would much rather have had a car, even a used one.

But that was also the year my parents got divorced, and I was trying hard to get along with both of them. I obediently went to the class at the YWCA in suburban Dallas, and I learned how to apply makeup and write thank-you notes and sit and stand gracefully. I did well enough that my teacher took me under her wing and encouraged me to do the beauty—I mean, scholarship—pageant circuit. This eventually led to my becoming what I sometimes refer to as a loser in Miss Texas competitions. Actually, I was in the top ten the final year I competed, which is pretty good news. The bad news was that's where I met my first husband, and the only reason he was interested in me was that I'd been in the competition. That isn't a good basis for a marriage. But that's another story.

What I did get out of all those pageants was what my parents wanted me to have: poise under fire. I may stumble around awkwardly in many of life's situations, but when the chips are down, I can pretend to handle things.

So when Joe caught me looking longingly into another man's eyes, I'm proud to say I coped. I pivoted just as if I'd been in the swimsuit competition, and said, "Joe! Great! Come on down and see the weird collection of books we've found."

I moved toward the stairs in what I hoped was a welcoming manner. If anybody jumped and looked guilty, it was Butch. I didn't look around to see how he was handling it. No, he was on his own.

Joe reacted with complete deadpan. Which was not a particularly good thing. When Joe gets completely deadpan, it usually means he's trying to hide what he's thinking. And I would have loved to know exactly what he'd seen and what he thought of it.

I certainly wasn't going to ask.

In the end, all three of us carried the situation off like adults. Joe came on down the steps, I greeted him, and I explained about the key. Butch showed him the books. And Joe smiled at the idea of Miss Vanderklomp hiding them.

Then he spoke. "Apparently she'd rather be suspected of murder than admit she hid these books."

"Joe!" I was aghast. "You can't mean she's a suspect in the death of Abigail Montgomery!"

"Also the death of Betty Blake. What else were Hogan and Larry Underwood supposed to think after she tried so hard to get into the basement? I don't know if finding these books will get her off the hook or not."

"Frankly, it seems like such a minor, well, crime. I'm not even sure it deserves that word. And why would she hurt either Abigail or Betty?"

"I'm speculating, Lee, but it would probably have been because they knew too much. Abigail obviously knew about the books, because she had the key to the closet. And it would have been easy for Betty to know as well, since she was in a hands-on position at the library."

I shook my head. "It's just so hard to visualize Miss Vanderklomp doing something like misapplying—I mean, misappropriating!—like misappropriating books. She's been such a moral force in Warner Pier for so long."

Butch was frowning. "She's been much too powerful for far too long."

Joe agreed. "Yes, to those of us who are her former students, she seemed to be a sort of joke, so we all let her get by with things. Does she have any legal authority with the library?"

"Not as far as I know," Butch said. "She's not on the library board. Of course, there's the Vanderklomp trust. It benefits the library."

"Who runs it?"

"I haven't had a chance to read the trust agreement yet."

I looked at Joe. "Did it come up when you were city attorney?"

"I don't remember anything about it. Butch, I could take a look at it, just informally. But I don't want to infringe on your authority."

"I'd be glad to share that chore."

Joe, Butch, and I left the basement with the books still scattered around, though we relocked the door to the hidden closet, and I gave the little brass key to Butch.

He locked the basement door. "I'll try to keep Miss Vanderklomp—and anybody else—out of the basement, but God knows who's got a key."

"Miss Vanderklomp said there were only two to the cabinet," I said.

Joe nodded. "But you said she told you she didn't know about the second one, so there could be more."

Butch looked through files in his office until he found one on the Vanderklomp trust. "Here's a copy of the trust agreement, and a financial report on the trust," he said. "Also minutes for a couple of meetings. I'd appreciate you looking at them."

Joe promised to return the documents the next day.

Then he turned to me. "Can you head over to Mom's office with me? We need to check on our insurance. Since your van is bound to be totaled."

There's a certain level of convenience in being married to the son of your insurance agent. Joe's mom assured us we could start shopping for a new vehicle; then I headed back to my office. I intended to collect pay for that workday, so I needed to put some time in there.

Through all of this looking at books, discussing library business, and walking down the street to his mom's office, Joe had maintained the same deadpan expression and behavior. He hadn't once said something like, "What the hell were you doing cheek to cheek and eye to eye with a new guy in town?" Or any other question that a husband is entitled to ask.

Of course, I had a come-back question all prepared. "What the hell were you doing in a lip lock with Meg Corbett right out on the street in front of your office?" And similar questions a wife has the right to ask.

Somehow we had maneuvered ourselves into a tit-for-tat situation, and apparently neither of us planned to bring the whole thing up. But Joe was still quiet. Not sullen. He never gets sullen. But it made me uneasy and I kept stumbling over my words. Usually when Joe and I are alone, I don't get my tang toungled. With him, I usually feel at ease.

In other words, we were both pretending everything was all right, and we both knew it wasn't. That's no way to live your life, even for a few hours.

When we got to my office, Joe didn't come in. But he told me he'd pick me up at five o'clock. And he squeezed my hand. It was better than nothing.

That evening we were finally alone—choosing food from the cafeteria in our refrigerator for dinner—but the phone rang several times. People were still checking on me, and we didn't talk a lot.

I told Joe I was well enough to load the dishwasher, and after that was done I worked on the leftover gift food for a while, putting things into smaller dishes and freezing things that could be frozen, plus making a list of who had brought what. Former contestants for Miss Texas always send handwritten thank-you notes.

By staying in the kitchen, I guess I was still trying to avoid the conversation we needed to have. When I left the kitchen Joe was sitting at the dining table, which doubles as a desk at our house. He was surrounded by papers.

"The Vanderklomp trust doesn't look complicated," he said.

Hmmm. Maybe Joe was trying to avoid that conversation, too.

He went on. "But I don't understand the financial statement."

"Who prepared it?"

"The only person who signed off was Miss Ann Vanderklomp."

"That doesn't sound right." I sat down at the table, and Joe handed me a sheaf of papers. I looked at them for a few minutes. "I'm not an auditor. All I can tell you is that the figures add up."

"But what's that grant to TAC?"

I read it again. "They gave ten thousand to the Warner Pier Public Library and five thousand to this TAC. Of course, this type of report doesn't have any information explaining what TAC is. There's no reason that it should. I mean, supporting data would be in a different document, and they might not give that to the library director."

Joe leaned back in his chair. "You know, I was city attorney for two years, and I never knew that this trust existed. It has no direct connection with the city legally."

"I guess that means that the city has no control over it."

"I suppose they don't have to. If the Vanderklomp family wants to put some money aside to benefit the library, of course they're free to do so. Unless they take the legal steps required to give the fund's principal to the city, the city doesn't have any responsibility for the money or its administration."

"Yes, but wouldn't the family have some tax benefits if they did it that way?"

"I'd think so. But I'm no tax attorney."

We both stared at the heap of papers. I sighed. "If

Butch Cassidy needs an auditor or a tax attorney to explain all this, he'd better call on two other people."

"Right."

Or, as it turned out, he could simply have read his mail.

Chapter 20

The next day was Sunday. Joe and I finally got our pancakes, but our breakfast conversation was stilted.

Around nine thirty I announced that I needed to go in to work. Joe said he wanted to repair the screen door; one-hundred-year-old houses are picturesque, but they require continuous upkeep. I drove myself to work in his truck and told him I'd come home at noon so he could go to the boat shop after lunch. I promised I'd be careful driving in, and that I'd keep the door to the shop locked while I was working.

I was determined to catch up on the work I had neglected the two previous days, beginning with the mail. The retail shop isn't open on Sundays after Labor Day, so I'd be on my own and could really get things done. Besides, sorting the mail seemed more productive than sitting around the house, cutting the tension with a knife.

When I got to my office, I found plenty of mail to

deal with. There was a pile left from the day I'd stayed home, plus the previous day's mail was sitting there, largely untouched. On that day I'd concentrated on e-mail and the bank deposit during the brief time I'd actually worked.

So I started making piles. Bills—there are always some of those. Orders—though many of our customers order by e-mail or by fax, there are still lots of mail orders for a business the size of ours. Then there were checks coming in—my favorite category, of course.

Finally there was a big pile of miscellaneous stuff. Sales letters. Newsletters. Begging letters. I had to open each one, read it or at least glance at it, and put it either into the appropriate stack or into the trash. It's amazing how much mail can go directly into the trash.

I was happy to see several envelopes containing checks. And even happier to receive a substantial order for chocolate Christmas items from a Chicago gift shop, and another nearly as large from a shop in Grand Rapids. I worked rapidly, fortifying myself with a cup of instant coffee and a chocolate malt truffle ("milk chocolate center with a milk chocolate coating, dusted with malt").

It was around ten thirty before I got through the orders, the bills, and the payments. Then I began to sort the miscellaneous mail.

I found the Warner Pier Chamber of Commerce newsletter and put it aside to read later. There was an invitation to a wine-and-cheese fund-raiser supporting a Grand Rapids women's shelter. I put it aside to decline and to send a small check. I support the shelter, but I'm not driving sixty miles for a glass of wine at my busiest time of the year. We don't have *that* many Grand Rapids customers I need to schmooze. Hope College had sent a reminder about a concert. I checked to make sure the date was already on my calendar.

So it went. There were more than a dozen similar items to be disposed of.

I was near the bottom of the stack before I found the plea from Camp Upright. I might have put it directly into the trash if the pitch from Brian Turley hadn't been so fresh in my mind. He'd made me curious about his camp, and now I wondered how his begging letters matched with his talk in our living room.

As I read the letter I almost yawned. Maybe it was because I'd heard the spiel recently, but Brian's material struck me as pretty dull. He had apparently sent the letter to the entire mailing list of the Warner Pier Chamber of Commerce, so it was impersonal. It explained the economic benefits of having the camp here, and those benefits didn't look all that big to me. He didn't have many employees, and all of them but him were seasonal. Almost all of them lived at the camp. The campers were kids without much money who were restricted from going to town. It sounded as if the main economic benefit of the camp was to Carol and Brian, not Warner Pier or Warner County, unless the C of C members felt strongly about developing character in the young through athletics. Personally, I have my doubts about that.

But I read it through, becoming more and more convinced I wasn't going to give them any money. Then I came to the information about where to send contributions.

At the top of the instructions, it said, "Make checks payable to TAC."

It took a moment for the three initials to sink in. Then I yelped. "TAC! Wow! Turley Athletic Camp!"

I was so excited I stood up and walked out of my office and all around the shop. But I kept staring at the begging letter.

TAC was the fund-raising arm of Brian Turley's camp?

The organization the Vanderklomp Foundation had given five thousand dollars?

But how could that foundation give money to a camp? The foundation supposedly had been established solely to benefit the Warner Pier Public Library.

Well, it could happen pretty easily if Miss Ann Vanderklomp wanted it to.

I reached for the phone. I wanted to tell somebody about this. Joe? He'd be excited. But our home phone rang ten times, and no one answered. So I tried his cell phone. No one answered it either.

Joe must be working outside, and he must not have put his phone in his pocket.

I tried to call Hogan, but again there was no answer. I remembered then that he and Aunt Nettie had planned to go to a picnic planned for Warner County law-enforcement officials by the county attorney. They were thirty miles away.

I decided that it wasn't vital that Hogan hear that information immediately, so I did not call 9-1-1 and request that the county dispatcher interrupt his social morning.

I told myself to calm down. Then I opened my computer and started on my e-mail. But I kept looking at the time, eager to call Joe or Hogan.

The knock on the outside door made me jump.

The shades on that door and on our show windows were down, so I couldn't see who was there. I toyed with the idea of not answering it, but I realized that the lights in my office were probably visible through the gaps around the shades. I might be snubbing someone I wanted to talk to.

But when I got to the door and pulled up the shade,

it wasn't anyone I wanted to see. On the other hand, it wasn't anyone who was likely to rob the store, either.

It was Miss Ann Vanderklomp, wearing a dressy navy blue dress with a white lace collar.

Everybody in Warner Pier knew that Miss Vanderklomp always went to the early service at the Episcopal church. Every day is casual day in Warner Pier, so most of us wear slacks or even jeans to church. I might have known Miss Vanderklomp would wear a dressy dress.

I hope I didn't roll my eyes like a teenager at the sight of her, though I sure wanted to. Besides, I'd begun to wonder how she found out I had that key.

I unlocked the door and opened it a few inches. "Yes, Miss Vanderklomp?"

"Good morning, Mrs. Woodyard. I saw your light and wondered if you were here. I hope you have changed your mind about giving me that key."

"No, I haven't. By the way, how did you know I had the key?"

Miss Vanderklomp rolled *her* eyes. "Oh, I have my methods. I know what's going on in Warner Pier."

I resisted the temptation to slam the door. I might have broken the glass. So I closed it gently, and Miss Vanderklomp walked away.

I went back to my computer, but my thoughts were completely disrupted. How *had* Miss Vanderklomp known I had that key? When she asked for it the day before I'd been so busy saying no that I hadn't wondered how she found that out.

I considered the question and came up with all sorts of possibilities.

She had seen me with it. No, that hadn't happened. I hadn't seen her between the time I got the key from Timothy Hart and the time she came to my office to confront me over it.

Maybe Timothy Hart had told her he gave it to me. No, I didn't believe that for a minute. The only person Tim had mentioned as having a legitimate interest in the key was Hogan. He would have had no reason to say anything to Miss Vanderklomp.

Maybe she had known where the key had been hidden, and she'd found out that Aunt Nettie and I had cleaned out Abigail Montgomery's refrigerator. That idea was stupid.

Nobody had seen the key after Tim gave it to me. He had handed it to me, and I had placed it beside the vase that held the roses he had brought. And Tim and Hart were the last visitors Joe and I had had the day after the van went off the bluff.

No, that was wrong. There were two more visitors: Carol and Brian Turley.

And Carol had taken an interest in the roses. While Joe and Brian had been getting coffee, Carol had commented on the roses. In fact, she could have seen me put Abigail's key in my pocket.

Aha! Carol Turley must have told Miss Vanderklomp that I had the key.

What was going on? Admittedly the key was distinctive, but Carol would have had to be familiar with one like it if she was going to recognize it.

Were Miss Vanderklomp and Carol in cahoots, joining forces to hide books they considered unsuitable for the library shelves?

That was silly. But the whole hiding-of-the-books thing was silly.

And what could that activity—reprehensible as it might be—have to do with the deaths of two people? Miss Vanderklomp might be embarrassed if her stash of books was publicly revealed, but that wouldn't be worth killing anybody over.

Actually, I told myself, Miss Vanderklomp probably wouldn't even be embarrassed if the whole thing came out. She undoubtedly saw her actions as perfectly justified and thought she had performed them for the good of the library.

And, again, how did Carol fit into the whole thing?

And who had killed Abigail Montgomery and Betty Blake? And why?

The only way I'd ever figure it out was if somebody captured the whole thing on a security camera. And the Warner Pier Public Library did not have security cameras.

That thought did remind me that I had taken a couple of pictures that I'd never shared with Hogan. I took one just after I discovered Betty Blake's body, and another before I started pulling the books off of her. I'd offered the photos to Hogan, but he'd said he'd look at them later. He hadn't seemed to think they were too important. The Michigan State Police lab techs had taken their own pictures.

I glanced at the office clock. In five minutes it would be eleven thirty, and I could again call Hogan and try to share the things I'd figured out. First, that Carol's husband's business had received money from the Vanderklomp trust. Second, that Carol had seen the key from Abigail's refrigerator—or I believed that she had—and had apparently told Miss Vanderklomp I had it. Third, the tale of the key and the hidden books; it might have nothing to do with the two deaths at the library, but Hogan should get a smile out of it.

Five minutes was just about the amount of time it would take for me to e-mail the two pictures from my phone to myself and to Hogan.

The photos downloaded smoothly, and I looked at the larger version on my computer screen. I shuddered at the sight of the books heaped on the floor, with poor Betty's worn shoes sticking out. At least the color had come out well—a miracle, considering the harsh shadows that crisscrossed the upstairs of the library. A red book on one of the tables almost glowed.

A red book? The object looked familiar. I blew up that section of the photo and looked at the rectangular red thing carefully.

It wasn't a book. It was a red folder. It was the red leather folder that Carol Turley carried with her to meetings. The one that held her reports and financial notes.

"Oh. My. Goodness," I said.

I quickly looked at the second photo, the one I had taken after I ran downstairs to call for help.

In that one the red folder was gone.

I sat at my desk, stunned.

Carol must have been in the adult section while I was wandering around, looking for Betty. When I ran downstairs to get help, she had grabbed her folder and slipped away down the back stairs.

Was there any other possible explanation?

I couldn't see one. Except . . . well, someone else might have had Carol's folder. But she never seemed to let it out of her sight. No, that folder was never far from Carol, so it was a logical assumption that she had brought it up to the adult section while the noisy kids' movie was playing downstairs. She must have gone up the back stairs, as well as escaping down them.

Carol must have killed Betty Blake.

And if she'd killed Betty, she had probably killed Abigail, too.

I shuddered. Then I hit SEND. I wanted somebody else, preferably Hogan, to have copies of those photos. Then I reached for the telephone and called Hogan's cell phone. I didn't care where he and Aunt Nettie were; I needed to talk to him, to tell him about Carol.

He didn't answer, of course. His phone was turned off. I left a "call me" message, but he might not get it for hours.

How dare Hogan not be at the phone, waiting eagerly for me to call and tell him the case was solved? I called the Warner Pier Police station. There the answering machine offered to link me up with the emergency operator. I hung up.

Then I called 9-1-1 and asked the operator if she could track Hogan down and give him an important message from his niece. But it was an operator I didn't know, and her reaction was unenthusiastic. I tried to make my message sound important, but I didn't want to share too much information. I wanted to talk to Hogan, not the 9-1-1 operator.

I called Joe again, thinking he might have a helpful idea, but he didn't answer.

I left a message on our phone and on Joe's cell phone.

Then I waited for Hogan to call me, stalking around the office like a madwoman and making guttural growls. I was still waiting half an hour later, at noon. That's when I decided to go home.

But when I got into Joe's truck, I discovered another frustration. The gas gauge was sitting on empty.

I growled again. I just wasn't in the mood to stop for gas.

But I did it. I drove to the station out on the highway, the one where Joe ordinarily gets gas, and I pumped a whole bunch of gasoline into the truck's huge fuel tank.

And while I was huddled between the truck and the gas pump, almost out of sight of the world, something interesting happened.

Miss Ann Vanderklomp pulled into the station in her two-year-old Buick and parked in one of the spots over by the mini mart. When she got out of the car I saw that she had changed out of her dressy navy blue dress. Now she wore denim slacks and—of all things—a gray Warner Pier High School sweatshirt.

I stared in surprise. Miss Vanderklomp in a sweatshirt and denim slacks? Strange. Then I told myself she probably planned to spend the afternoon raking leaves or doing some other autumn chore. Even Miss Vanderklomp would occasionally have to do some physical labor to get along in life.

She was in the little shop only a few minutes, and when she came out, she carried a small sack. I was surprised to see her open the trunk to put it inside.

I was even more surprised to see that the trunk was already loaded.

Even from thirty feet away I could see what was in the trunk of the Buick. It was loaded with flat pieces of cardboard.

Boxes. Unassembled boxes. And I knew immediately what she was going to do with them.

Chapter 21

To me it was obvious what was going on. Miss Vanderklomp was going to pack up those books in the basement of the library and carry them away.

I got so excited I nearly knocked the nozzle of the gas pump out of the tank. I didn't know what to do. I seem to remember running back and forth—as much as possible when I was jammed in between a gas pump and a large pickup—trying to figure out how to handle this.

Then the gas pump clicked off. I collected my receipt—accountants do this sort of thing even when excited—and got in the truck. Then I followed Miss Vanderklomp.

She was driving at half the speed limit and swerving a bit now and then. It was easy to catch up with her. I had plenty of time to consider both her actions and what I should do about them.

First, could she get into the library's basement to get the books? I was sure Butch had locked the basement door, but somehow I was willing to bet she had a set of keys of her own. Second, did it matter if she took the books? I decided that it did. Those books were library property.

So I ought to tell Butch Cassidy about it. But before I did that I'd better make sure that was what was going on. I'd feel like an idiot if Miss Vanderklomp went home and used those boxes to pack up old clothes for the Salvation Army.

I continued to follow her light blue Buick through the quiet streets of Warner Pier. To my surprise, she didn't drive directly to the library. She drove instead to the Independent Fellowship, a nondenominational church. It took me a few seconds to picture a map of Warner Pier and to realize that the church was on the street *behind* the library. She was approaching the library from the rear.

This looked more and more like book theft.

I drove on by the church, blessing the fact that Joe's truck had tinted windows. I didn't think Miss Vanderklomp could see me through them, and she probably wouldn't recognize the truck, even though it had been sitting in front of TenHuis Chocolade when she stopped in. At least she hadn't mentioned it. She had said she came to the door because she saw there was a light on.

A lot of people in Warner Pier know my van because it's the only one in town with a Dallas Cowboys bumper sticker, but Joe is an M-Go-Blue fan, and there are dozens of pickups around with University of Michigan stickers.

The Independent Fellowship building sits on a city lot in our old-fashioned downtown area, and two or three lots adjoining it have been cleared for parking. The parking areas—in fact, the whole church property—were empty. Apparently the Independent Fellowship services are over early.

Miss Vanderklomp drove around behind the church. This gave me a problem, because I couldn't see what she was doing back there.

I went on to the end of the block and turned right. I found a parking place next to the alley. Then I got out and walked down the alley toward the church and library. The alley had businesses on either side. All of them were closed. I didn't see a soul as I approached the library and church.

When I got close to the spot where Miss Vanderklomp had parked, I came to the parking lot of the Elite Beauty Salon. This lot was edged by a big hedge, and by hiding behind it I was able to see the area behind the church. I sure hoped the gal who ran the Elite wasn't there. She would have wondered about this odd woman roaming around on her property.

The area behind the church was just what I'd expected. There were two or three parking spots, probably used by the staff and deliverymen. And two vehicles were parked in them.

The first, of course, was Miss Vanderklomp's light blue Buick. The other was a dirty white van.

Carol Turley was standing beside the van. There was a rectangle of cleaner paint on its front door, and I was willing to bet that a magnetic sign that read CAMP UPRIGHT usually marked that spot.

Then Miss Vanderklomp came out from behind her car. To my surprise, she staggered and almost fell.

Carol took her arm. When she spoke I could hear her voice clearly. "Oh, Miss Vanderklomp, I believe you're ill. Let me help you across to the library."

"I'm just tired, terribly tired," Miss Vanderklomp said. "But I must get those books packed up."

"I'll help you across. Then I'll come back for the boxes."

They started across the alley, with Miss Vanderklomp leaning heavily on Carol's arm. She had her purse looped over her left shoulder, and she clutched her water bottle in her right hand.

There was a certain amount of fumbling, but either Carol or Miss Vanderklomp had a key, and they went in the back door of the library.

I turned and ran back down the alley to the truck. It was time to call in the cavalry.

As soon as I was in the truck, I grabbed my cell phone and started trying to get hold of people. I called information for a new number for Henry Cassidy. Or for Butch Cassidy. No listing under either name. I used my phone to find Rhonda Ringer-Riley's number. If Butch was renting a house from her, she ought to have his phone number. Rhonda didn't answer. I called Joe. He didn't answer. I growled in frustration.

I once again tried both of Hogan's phones. He didn't answer either.

Where was everybody?

Finally, I called my mother-in-law. Since Mercy is married to a restaurant owner, he's extra busy on weekends, and she's usually home. Sure enough, she answered.

"Thank God!" I said. "A human voice!"

"Lee? What's wrong?"

"Mercy, will you get on the phone and call Joe? Or else drive out to the house and find him? I can't raise him."

"What?"

"He's got to be home. I'm driving his truck."

"He's probably outside. Can't you just keep calling? What's the emergency?"

"Listen, Mercy. I'm in the alley behind the Independent Fellowship Church. Their services are over, and the lot is empty except for the cars of Miss Ann Vanderklomp and Carol Turley. I think the two of them are stealing books from the library."

"Stealing books? Miss Vanderklomp? Oh, Lee . . ."

"But that's not the scary part. I think Carol Turley killed Abigail Montgomery and Betty Blake."

"Carol? But she's the treasurer of the Warner Pier Lecture Club!"

"I don't care if she's treasurer of the Virtue Society of America. I think she killed both of them. And now she and Miss Vanderklomp are alone at the library, and I think Carol's ready to kill her, too!"

Mercy gasped.

I almost yelled out the next words. "Miss Vanderklomp is staggering! I'm sure she's been drugged. I'm relying on you, Mercy. We need to find Hogan. And Joe can usually do that. So you find Joe! Now!" I almost hung up. Then I remembered the other important part. "I'm calling 9-1-1, but Joe might find Hogan faster! And Hogan can get action!"

I punched the phone off. Then I got out of the truck. If only I had some sort of weapon. Well, maybe I did. I was driving Joe's truck, after all, and in the bed of it was a big toolbox.

I opened the toolbox and poked around to see what Joe had in there. Unfortunately most of his tools looked pretty harmless. I wasn't about to attack a murderer with a paintbrush.

I finally found a medium-sized hammer. I stuck the handle down the front of my shirt and hung the head on my bra. This wasn't either attractive or comfortable, but at least it kept my hands free. Then I reached into the glove box and pulled out a large flashlight.

I started walking toward the church, and as I walked I took out my phone and punched in 9-1-1.

I told the emergency operator that I had reason to believe that two unauthorized people had broken into the Warner Pier Public Library.

"The public library?" She was incredulous.

"You may recall there have been two suspicious deaths there within the last week," I said.

"I thought those were accidents."

"Suspicious deaths." I said the words firmly. "If you don't get some cops here, there may be another."

"Now, Mrs. Woodyard—"

"I'm not threatening to hurt anybody. I'm trying to stop any more mayhem. Police Chief Hogan Jones and Inspector Larry Underwood of the state police are in charge of the investigation. Please inform them."

"Where are you?"

"I'm going in the back door of the library, following the suspicious people who are already in there. Please get someone here ASAP. This is an emergency."

I hung up.

Immediately my phone rang. I looked at the number calling. It was the 9 1 1 operator calling back. I answered the phone and said, "Call Hogan. Now!" Then I turned the phone off and put it in my pocket.

I walked on. I tried to be quiet as I approached the back door of the library. And I was lucky. It was not locked.

Or I guess I was lucky. I didn't understand why it wasn't locked. Carol had been the last person through it, and in her place I would have locked it as soon as I was inside. But she'd had her hands full holding up Miss Vanderklomp.

I opened the door and crept inside. The flashlight immediately became important. The door led into that

tiny back hall, and after the outside door swung closed
that hall was pitch-black. I tried to remember the layout
of the hall, though I'd only been in it once. A door in
front of me, I believed, opened into the workroom at
the back of the downstairs stacks. A door to the left led
to stairs down to the basement.

I felt for the handle of the basement door and opened
it. To my surprise, it was just as dark in the basement
as it was in the back hall. I shone the light from the
flashlight down the stairs to make sure it was the basement.

What was going on? I had been positive that Miss
Vanderklomp and Carol had come to pack up the stash
of books. So if they hadn't gone to the basement, where
had they gone?

Maybe Carol couldn't get Miss Vanderklomp down
those steep stairs. Maybe she'd taken her into the library's workroom.

I felt for the door in front of me, turned the handle,
and eased it open.

I was looking into another pit of blackness. It was
hard to realize that outside was a bright, sunny day.
The inside of the library appeared to have absorbed all
existing light.

Did I dare use the flashlight? I decided I had to. I
couldn't walk across that crowded workroom in the
dark without falling over something and either breaking my neck or making such a noise that Carol would
know I was there. So I turned on the flashlight and
made my way across the workroom, being careful not
to fall over a chair or kick a table or shove a rolling rack
into something that would rattle or bang.

When I got within arm's reach of the door into the
reading room, I turned off the flashlight. And I turned
the door handle gently and peeked out.

Light. Thank goodness there was light.

Not a lot of light. But the big room I was looking into did have windows at one end. It was dim in there, but it did have light.

I was behind some of the stacks, so I still couldn't see much. I slipped into the room, closed the door behind me, and began to explore.

One thing you've got to give a library: There are lots of places to hide. And you don't even have to poke your head around the ends of the shelves. No, nearly everywhere I could find spaces over the tops of the books. These made slits that allowed me to see at least into the next aisle.

I crept along, making sure I didn't knock into anything or trip over one of the step stools. I was heading for the center of the room, where there was a seating area. It seemed to be the most logical place for Miss Vanderklomp to be, the place where Carol would have led her. The danger was that Carol might have stashed Miss Vanderklomp there, but herself be roaming around the room. I might come face-to-face with her. And she might have a gun or a knife, while all I had was a hammer.

Then I heard this strange noise. It was a sort of grinding noise, followed by a hiss.

I kept moving toward the center of the room, creeping along, peeking through the shelves. And listening to that grind-hiss noise, I wondered if it were an animal of some sort. A hog? Was that grinding sound a snort?

Then I came to the children's section. All of a sudden I was taller than the shelves were. I dropped to my knees and began to crawl toward the seating area. At the end of the shelf, where a wider aisle separated the ranks of shelving, I reared up on my knees and peeked through the books. I could see directly into the seating area.

Carol was nowhere in sight. But lying on the couch was Miss Ann Vanderklomp. And I understood the noise I'd been hearing. Miss Vanderklomp was snoring.

Her snores weren't the timid, ladylike sort, either. She was belting them out—snorts and hisses and whistles.

I leaned against the Eric Carle books and laughed. How humiliated Miss Vanderklomp would be if she ever learned she'd been caught snoring! I didn't dare make a sound, but I was simply dying to roll on the floor over the ridiculous situation.

Except that it wasn't really funny. I felt positive that Carol had drugged Miss Vanderklomp. Perhaps she was staging a suicide.

Where was Carol? I couldn't see her anywhere, and I couldn't hear her.

Of course, if Carol had already staged the suicide scene, she might have left the building. I hadn't seen her go out the back door, but it was possible she'd crept out while I was crawling around peeking through bookshelves.

Just as I began to feel hopeful, all hell broke loose.

I heard a noise behind me and I turned to find myself face-to-face with Carol.

She came around the end of the bookshelf behind me and stopped as if I'd hit her with a paralysis ray of some sort. She seemed to be frozen, standing at the end of the bookshelf I was kneeling behind.

Then we both moved. I reached for the hammer I had stuffed down my shirt, and Carol grabbed a large, flat book from the top shelf. She got her weapon first. Holding the book in both hands, she swung it at me the way a street fighter would swing a two-by-four.

I ducked. A bra does not make a very good holster,

and I was having trouble with my quick draw. The hammer was tangled with my undies.

Carol swung twice, and I kept ducking. I managed to avoid being hit in the head. I was still on my knees, and I launched myself at her, hitting her with a tackle that justified that Dallas Cowboys sticker my van flaunted.

She went down like a dead tree in a high wind, right over on her backside, landing on her fanny with a shock that shook the floor of the ancient building.

Then she got one foot free and kicked at me. The two of us grappled on the floor, twisting and wrestling. Carol began shrieking, and I was grunting. We must have been a real spectacle. I remember seeing Miss Vanderklomp in the distance and thinking that she was missing a show.

Then something hard hit my jaw. Later I decided it must have been Carol's foot; she had kicked me. I lost my hold on her. For a moment I couldn't seem to move. A hard rod was pressing against my breastbone, for one thing.

It was that hammer. My secret weapon.

The thought energized me, and I climbed to my feet, ignoring the aches and pains left from the van's trip down the bluff. I finally got the hammer out.

And I realized that Carol was getting away. She was running down the aisle toward the front desk, and, beyond it, the front door.

"No!" I screamed.

And I threw the hammer at her.

Luckily, it missed. If it had hit her, it might have killed her, and I'd just as soon not live with that. But, no, the hammer went over her head and hit the glass in the front door. The glass must have been safety glass, because it shattered into a million tiny pieces, but stayed inside its frame. Carol gave another shriek, and I roared like an angry mother bear.

Beside me was a book cart, the type that rolls, with shelves on either side. I yanked it out into the aisle, aimed it more carefully than I had the hammer, and sent it flying.

It hadn't even begun to slow down when it hit Carol full in the back. She fell headlong into the front door. The front door flew open, and Carol landed in the arms of Butch Cassidy. And Joe.

I ran to the door. Joe and Butch Cassidy stood there, each holding one of Carol's arms.

There was a lot more yelling and screaming as three state policemen ran up. Then Hogan finally got there. And Jerry Cherry, his main patrolman.

I was still yelling. "Call the EMTs!"

"Why?" Joe had the presence of mind to be sardonic. "Are they the only people missing?"

I pointed to the couch.

"Oh, my God!" Joe said.

Miss Vanderklomp had slept through the excitement. She gave a loud grunt and followed it with a wheeze.

I collapsed into a chair near her.

"What a day," I said.

Chapter 22

The mayhem stopped then, but the excitement was far from over.

Carol made a brief try at convincing everyone I had been the aggressor, but that didn't go very far. It seems that the owner of the Elite Beauty Salon actually had been in her building, catching up on chores. She'd seen Carol help Miss Vanderklomp across the alley and into the library. She'd seen me go back and forth down the alley, talking on my cell phone as I frantically tried to get law enforcement there. Of course, my phone records proved whom I'd been calling.

But Carol's nerve broke after a hospital representative called to say Miss Vanderklomp had been drugged, but the doctors felt sure she would survive. And Hogan took Miss Vanderklomp's bottle to test the Pepsi inside for drugs. We all knew that a surviving Miss Vanderklomp would confirm that she had not attempted suicide, and possibly would even reveal that Carol had poured Pepsi into her bottle.

When Carol heard that, she began to cry. "I had to save Brian's camp," she said.

Then Carol began to confess. It was only after somebody whispered the word "lawyer" in her ear that she shut up. But Hogan said it wasn't hard to figure out what had happened.

Brian and Carol were broke.

Five years earlier, Brian was a middle-school phys ed teacher with an idea for a camp. More than a camp; a chain of camps. He met Carol when he came to look at the camp she'd inherited, with an eye toward renting it.

My cynical nature suspects he found it easier to marry the camp than to rent it. At any rate he and Carol opened Camp Upright.

But both of them should have kept their day jobs. The camp never made money. Gradually Carol grew desperate. And as far as I can tell, Carol never shared the financial problems with Brian. Maybe she was afraid that if he gave up on the camp, he'd leave her, too.

His camp and his scheme to build a chain of such camps seemed to be all Brian cared about. Joe and I had witnessed his offhand treatment of Carol.

But Brian was everything to Carol. She worshipped him. If his camp failed, Carol would not only lose her inheritance, but she would also lose her husband.

Meanwhile, Carol was treasurer for five different community organizations. Any small-town citizen will recognize this situation; I call it the Work a Willing Horse to Death syndrome. The people who are willing to do the jobs get elected.

Several of these organizations didn't have proper safeguards on handling their funds. The temptation was too much for Carol. She began to rifle their accounts.

The library board, with its setup under state law and its limited say in how city funds were spent, had not fallen victim.

Carol had snuck down to the basement to figure out why Miss Vanderklomp kept going down there. It didn't take long for her to figure out that Miss Vanderklomp was hiding books in her special closet. Then Carol figured out a way to use that knowledge.

Miss Vanderklomp isn't going to explain to the world at large, but Carol must have convinced her she supported the effort to keep the library shelves untainted by reading material that lacked intellectual content. Then Carol asked for a grant to Brian's camp.

Abigail Montgomery must also have been curious about Miss Vanderklomp's trips to the basement. Plus, she looked at the Vanderklomp Foundation financial report, which was a public document. I'm guessing that she followed Carol to the basement to confront her about the donation to TAC.

Abigail wound up dead. Carol dragged her body to the foot of the stairs, hoping to make it look as if she had fallen.

Betty Blake had told me she had found something odd in the library's financial records. Hogan believes that it was the grant to TAC in the Vanderklomp trust. When Betty called me, probably to ask me, as an accountant, about the legality of this, Carol somehow discovered Betty was suspicious. She knocked her out with a volume of the Encyclopaedia Britannica, then finished the job with repeated blows from the book. Then she shoved the bookshelf over, dumping hundreds of books on Betty, trying to make her death look accidental.

When the state police technicians searched Carol's home—Brian gave them permission—they found a pair of slacks and some shoes with blood on them. Yes, it matched Betty's.

But after she killed Betty, before Carol could flee down the back stairs, I had happened upon the scene. Carol didn't realize I had taken photographs; she was simply afraid I had seen the red folder. So she later enticed me to the dangerous stretch of road and pushed me and my van down the bluff. Another supposed accident, but I was lucky.

Carol was smart enough not to use either her car or the camp's van for this, of course. She used a large SUV that had been donated to the camp as part of its fund-raising efforts. Some people gave boats; some cars. One of them had paint on it that matched my poor wrecked van.

Brian seemed stunned by the whole thing. I finally concluded that he was about as intelligent as a rutabaga and never caught on to what Carol was doing. He'd been leaving the finances entirely up to her.

The saddest part may have been that by the end of the afternoon, Brian was telling everyone in sight that he knew nothing about what Carol had been up to.

"I'm just a dupe," he said.

"Dope" might have been a better word. A few remarks supporting his wife might have sounded good.

Butch made sure the books were out of the basement closet before Miss Vanderklomp was out of the hospital. He says she never mentioned their existence to him, and he didn't ask her about them. The books were simply moved to the new library. Some were added to the collection, and some were not. But now Warner Pier girls can check out any book from a complete set of 1960s vintage Nancy Drew mysteries.

Later Hogan told Joe and me that the state police lab techs, in searching the basement, had found the hidden closet the night that Abigail Montgomery was killed.

"Did they get into it?" I asked.

"Sure," he said. "They have lots ways to open old locks. The problem was, it was just an old closet in the basement of an old library. So finding it full of old books didn't make anybody too excited. They looked in there, then locked it up again."

I laughed. "If Miss Vanderklomp had just ignored that closet, the whole thing would have gone away. But once Carol realized that Miss Vanderklomp didn't want anyone to know what she had been doing, she had a hold on her."

"Right," Hogan said. "Carol must have convinced her that she could be an ally in the book-censoring project—if she got a little money for her trouble."

"But Abigail Montgomery must have figured out what was going on," I said. "I wonder where she got her key."

"Her key was a copy made by that old locksmith in Holland. We surmise that Mrs. Montgomery suspected something funny was going on and that it centered on that closet. When she got temporary possession of the key—maybe Miss Vanderklomp dropped it or something—she had a copy made."

Hogan chuckled. "Have you guessed why the closet was built in the first place?"

"I suppose the Vanderklomp grocers used it."

"But what for?"

I frowned, and Joe began to laugh. "Prohibition!"

"Right!" Hogan said. "The Vanderklomps ran their store all during Prohibition, and if we had any way to check, I bet old Mr. Vanderklomp had a private stock of booze imported from Canada for a few regular customers. That's one of those things the respectable Miss Vanderklomp would probably not want brought up today."

I'm certainly not going to ask her about it.

As for how my résumé and Butch's letter—I figured out it was from his father, who was still in prison—got under Abigail's body, well, apparently Carol carried them down to the basement. Joe believes she was looking at the things on Butch's desk—just because she was nosy—when Abigail confronted her. Carol probably suggested they talk someplace private, and the basement would fit the bill. When Abigail made it clear she was going to tell about the books in the hidden closet, Carol was afraid the illegal donation to Brian's camp was going to come out. She picked up the nearest blunt instrument and let Abigail have it.

Butch said there had been a chartreuse pencil on his desk, something left by the previous library director. Where Mrs. Smith got it, I have no idea, but Carol apparently carried that downstairs as well.

Most of those things took us weeks to figure out. Luckily, Joe and I were able to settle our personal problems that very day.

It was late afternoon when we left the police station and headed home. As we turned into our drive, Joe spoke. "Why don't you get a jacket, and we'll go down to watch the sunset? We need a little peace and quiet, and there shouldn't be anybody at the beach now."

Sure enough, when we got to the lake our little stretch of Lake Michigan access was deserted. We spread out a double-sized beach towel to sit on. Since the beach faces west, we were looking directly into the sunset.

It was gloriously purple, orange, pink, and gray, with just enough clouds to keep the sun from glaring in our eyes. The breeze was brisk, making it cool enough that I wasn't surprised when Joe sat close to me and put his arm around my shoulders. I was surprised when he took two deep breaths and said, "Listen, Lee."

He might as well have made an announcement. "I have something important to say."

It took one more deep breath before he got down to business. "I wanted to tell you what's going on with Meg."

"Joe, I won't demand . . ."

"No, I want to explain. When it first came up, I didn't understand it, so I didn't give a very good reason for seeing her. But that day you spent under the influence of pain pills, I pretty much figured out what's going on. I think."

He took another deep breath. "You and my mom have always acted as if Meg had this mysterious hold on me, as if she had cast a spell over me."

"That's silly, Joe."

"Yes, it's silly. But you may have been right. I never saw it, because there was a part of the story you and Mom didn't know about."

He took another deep breath. "When I was sixteen, Meg just about destroyed any confidence I had about dealing with women." He needed two deep breaths before he could go on. "I don't know how to be delicate about this."

I wasn't eager to hear that Joe had been intimate with Meg. "You don't need to tell me all the details, Joe."

"Thanks. Anyway, the next day—the very next day—she dropped me."

I didn't know whether I should laugh or cry, so I didn't do either. I just slid my arm around Joe's waist and leaned my head into the curve of his neck. I could imagine how devastating an experience like that would be for a young guy, one having his first real sexual experience.

"I was crushed," Joe said. "I felt as if I must have

been the most inept— Well, it seems ridiculous now, but at the time, it pretty much knocked me in a heap."

"Were you in love with her, Joe?"

"I was in love with her on a sixteen-year-old's level, Lee. When you're thirty-five, the way you felt then seems stupid."

I remembered the real reason I'd been so upset about moving from Prairie Creek to Dallas when I was sixteen. "I was in love when I was that age," I said, "and it's sure serious at the time."

"Sure is. Anyway, life went on, I recovered, and, I'm afraid, for a while I fully regained my confidence. Then I married Clemmie, and of all the problems we had, bed wasn't one of them."

I already knew that. Joe's first wife had been crazy about him on a physical level, and I knew he had found her sexy, too. I've always had a feeling that their ill-advised marriage had lasted the few years it did last because of great sex. I'm okay with that. I'd been married before, too, and I was strongly attracted to my first husband. But like Joe, I discovered that physical attraction doesn't last if mutual respect is gone.

When Joe and I found each other, it was a whole new start for both of us.

"Anyway," Joe said, "I thought I had gotten over Meg completely. I hadn't given her a thought in years. Oh, after she and Trey moved back to Warner Pier, I might run into her at the post office, but I could deal with it. Then she popped up in our lives four years ago when Trey decided I was blocking his ambitions, and we had all that trouble over Hershel Perkins."

"I admit I was happy when Meg left town."

"And I admit I was, too. I just didn't want to fool with her. But I guess deep down, my sixteen-year-old's pride was still hurt. That's my only excuse for what happened when she turned up two weeks ago."

"Two weeks ago?"

"Yes, she called me at the office. She said she was establishing residence in Holland so she could get a divorce, and she asked if I could help her with it. She's working as a hostess at the yacht club. She asked me to come out for lunch and discuss the case."

Yet another deep breath. This wasn't an easy story for Joe to tell. "You don't need to tell me that the smart thing to do would have been to refer her to another attorney," he said.

"Joe, if she didn't have any money—and hostessing in a restaurant doesn't sound like a high-paying job— then that's what your agency does."

"Yeah, but there are three other attorneys in the agency. I could have told her one of them could help her. So the lunch at the yacht club was a bad idea. The other lunch and the dinners were worse ideas."

He turned toward me and added his second arm to the one he already had around me. "And that's all, Lee. All we did was eat."

I laughed. "I never doubted that, Joe. Somehow I've never been afraid that you'd go to bed with Meg. I've always been afraid that you were still in love with her."

"No! Lee, you don't have to worry about that! At this point I'm pretty sure I've never been in love with her. Not even when I was sixteen. In fact, I've spent the past three days trying to figure out why I agreed even to speak to her. And I think I finally came up with an explanation."

"You don't have to explain anything."

"After all this thought and analysis? I may write a paper on it."

After we'd laughed, I took his hand. "Okay. Let's hear this historic explanation."

"I wanted to get even with her."

"And giving her dinner did this? The food must have been awful."

Joe kissed my cheek. "Be serious when I'm sharing my inmost feelings, please!"

"Sorry."

"After a lot of deep thought, I realized that I was still mad at Meg because she dropped me—nearly twenty years ago. What I was doing was building her up for the big push. To get even."

"And did you?"

"Well, no. I didn't drop her the way she dropped me. But yesterday I told her I was going to be really busy, so I was turning her case over to Susan Gilson."

"Susan does family law anyway, doesn't she?"

"We all do. But I'm pretty much ashamed of myself."

"Why? It sounds as if you handled it fine."

"The end result may have been the same, but admitting that my main motive was revenge . . . it doesn't make me proud of myself."

"What about all this stuff you handed out about how *good* women like your mother—and me!—just wouldn't give Meg a chance?"

"That's what I kept telling myself. That it wasn't Meg's fault."

"What wasn't Meg's fault?"

"Her character, I guess. The way she uses people. Uses her . . . her appeal to get her way. Look at poor old Trey. She went for him because he came from a prominent family. The poor guy was putty in her hands. When she found out his family was prominent, but not rich, well, that relationship was doomed."

Joe squeezed me. "Anyway, I'm over Meg for good. You and my mother can relax."

"I never doubted that you'd come to your senses. And you figured all this out the day I was on pain pills?"

"You told me all your secrets, too."

"Oh." That's what I said out loud. What I was thinking was, Gosh! I hope I didn't tell *all* of them.

"Yeah," Joe said. "And, by the way, maybe you should turn down that appointment to the library board."

I gasped. Darn! He knew how I felt about Butch Cassidy.

I felt his body shake, and I realized he was laughing. At me.

"You rat!" I gave Joe a huge shove, and he fell over backward, landing with his head off the edge of the towel.

I leaned over, glaring at him. "Here I was, having these massive attacks of guilt, and you thought it was funny." Then I had to laugh, too.

Joe gently tugged me down on top of him. "That was the day I discovered that any time I need to know what's going on in that beautiful blond head, all I have to do is sock a little codeine to you. It's just like truth serum." He gave me a long kiss. "Don't worry. Even when you were rambling around in La-La Land, I could tell it was just a daydream." Another kiss. Or several.

Finally he spoke again. "Anyway, I can see that Butch is an attractive guy. Like you always tell me, I don't want you to lose interest." He gave me a serious kiss. "And I promise to hold all future business conferences in the office." Another kiss. "And I have complete confidence in your behavior. But in the future, I'd appreciate it if you didn't explore old basements. You might stumble across some temptation there."

"I already promised that, Joe. At the same time you did." I didn't have to mention our wedding date.

After a little more necking, I sat up. "We'd better quit this. After all, this is a public beach. And we've missed the sunset."

"There'll be another one tomorrow." Joe climbed to his feet. "Let's go home, Lee."

Read on for an excerpt from JoAnna Carl's
latest Chocoholic Mystery,

THE CHOCOLATE CLOWN CORPSE

Available now in hardcover from Obsidian.

I don't usually answer the telephone at the Warner Pier police station.

Warner Pier is a small town, true, and my aunt is married to the police chief, true, and somehow I wind up at the station now and then. But the PD has staff—the chief, four patrolmen, and a clerical assistant. The 9-1-1 calls go to a county system twenty-four hours a day, and after the office closes at five o'clock, ordinary business calls are caught by an answering machine after two rings.

They don't need a volunteer to answer the phone in Warner Pier, Lake Michigan's most picturesque resort.

But that day I was sitting around the station at five fifteen, the only person there, waiting for my aunt and uncle and my husband so we could all go out to dinner. I had plopped into a chair next to the empty desk usually occupied by the secretary. When the phone rang my mind was in three other places, and after just one ring, I automatically picked up the phone.

"TenHuis Chocolade," I said.

I'd not only answered a phone I shouldn't have. I'd answered it the way I do for my job.

The caller, a woman, spoke uncertainly. "Oh! I was calling the Warner Pier Police Department."

"And you reached it. I'm not the regular person who answers the phone, so I said the wrong thing. But I'll try to help you."

"Oh. Well . . ." The caller had an odd, whispery voice. "I wanted to ask about a crime that happened about a month ago."

"I can refer your question to the right person."

"It was a violent death."

Hmmm. Warner Pier doesn't have all that many killings. Or did she mean an accident? "Yes?"

"The murder of Morris Davidson. The clown. A month ago. Do you remember it?"

"Oh, yes. It caused quite a stir around town." I looked at the caller ID on the secretary's phone. The little screen held a number with an area code I didn't recognize. "Where are you calling from? I'm surprised the Davidson killing got any attention outside of Warner County, since it was not too unusual."

She didn't answer my question. "Not unusual? Why do you say that?"

"It was the proverbial break-in with the burglar reacting violently when surprised by the homeowner."

The caller gasped. "Is that what people think happened?"

"After the confession, there wasn't much else to think."

"Confession? You mean someone confessed to the murder?"

"Yes. He's now in jail."

"Oh." I could barely hear her. The woman's voice

was more than surprised. It was amazed. Maybe beyond amazed.

"Who is this?" I asked.

She spoke but again didn't answer my question. "In jail! But that's awful!"

"It's pretty standard procedure," I said. "If you confess to killing someone, you are sent to jail. Can you give me your name?"

The only answer was a click as the woman hung up.

I stared at the silent receiver. "Weird," I said.

There was a knock at the door, and I looked up to see my husband, Joe, through its window. I let him in and immediately told him about the phone call.

"Isn't that strange?" I asked.

Joe shrugged. "You say there was no name on the caller ID?"

"Right. There was a number, but no name. Is that suspicious?"

"Not necessarily." Joe was a lawyer and his office was in the same building as the police station. So he's drunk a lot of coffee with cops.

"The call was probably made from a pay phone," he said. "There are still a few around."

"But the woman sounded so amazed to learn a burglar had confessed to killing Moe Davidson."

"We were all astonished, as I recall."

"I admit I was."

Joe grinned. "Lee, when the guy everybody loves to hate is murdered, every single person in town is a suspect. So finding out that Moe was taken out by someone who didn't even know him—well, Agatha Christie wouldn't have approved."

Joe sat down in one of the visitors' chairs and picked up a magazine. "So I tend to agree with your caller."

"What do you mean?"

"Just that the whole situation was astonishing. Not satisfying." Joe looked into space for a moment before he spoke again. "Frankly, I don't think the guy— Hollis? Is that his name? I don't think he had good representation. If I were his attorney, that confession would never have been made, much less accepted as true."

He gave a short laugh. "Although he'd probably still be right where he is now. In jail. And he may yet be sent for a decent mental examination."

My uncle and aunt Hogan and Nettie Jones arrived then, and the four of us went out to dinner. I told Hogan about the odd phone call, but he simply shrugged.

"Some curious person. But Davidson's death was surprising all around. His whole life was surprising."

"Surprising how?"

"First off, how could such an annoying guy be so funny?"

When the caller had called Moe Davidson a clown, she hadn't been slamming his intelligence or personality. Moe had literally been a clown. He'd dressed up in a comic hobo outfit and marched in parades under the name "Hobo Moe." He had done pantomime jokes. He'd pulled quarters out of kids' ears. He'd walked an invisible dog.

Moe had even run a clown business, Clowning Around, which happened to be located in the shop next door to TenHuis Chocolade, where I'm business manager.

Moe's store offered clown paraphernalia and collectibles—dolls, games, costumes, DVDs, figurines, notepaper, and a million other items. He had provided a clown act for parties. Anything to do with clowns was available at his store.

But Moe had been equally well-known in Warner Pier for his nonclown activities. When he hadn't been funny, Moe had been one of the most annoying cranks in town. At one time or another—when he hadn't been wearing his clown outfit—all of us could cheerfully have killed him, or at least yelled at him.

As far as I know, Moe Davidson had never hit, stabbed, shot, drowned, or otherwise physically attacked anyone. But, by golly, he had hurt a lot of people.

Moe's weapon had been his tongue. He could figure out where anyone's sensitive spot was, and he had known just what to say to make that sensitive spot hurt. He had whacked my ego with a verbal crowbar every time he walked into TenHuis Chocolade, and he seemed to walk in there a lot more than I wanted him to.

I have this problem talking. I mix up my words. The highfalutin name for it is "malapropism," named after a Mrs. Malaprop in an eighteenth-century play. She made *Bartlett's Familiar Quotations* for describing a fellow character as "headstrong as an allegory on the banks of the Nile."

I once remarked that an unusually kind person had "lots of apathy." Personally, I don't find Mrs. Malaprop very funny. To me the condition is embarrassing, not humorous.

I control this most of the time; it comes out mainly when I'm nervous. And I never once spoke to Moe Davidson without feeling nervous. He laughed whenever he saw me. That made me nervous, and I misspoke.

Once he had come into TenHuis Chocolade for a pound of truffles, and I recommended the "Asexual Spice—I mean, *Asian* Spice!" Another time, he had approached me with a formal document he wanted to present to the Warner Pier City Council, and I said, "Oh, I'm sorry. I make it a rule not to sign petit fours—I mean, petitions!"

Moe would laugh at me and tell everybody in town

what I'd said. He became the only person in Warner Pier I actively tried to avoid. And I couldn't avoid him, since he worked next door. When he wasn't too busy with civic affairs to open the store.

When Joe was serving as city attorney, he couldn't avoid him either. Moe Davidson had been that annoying citizen who got up at every civic meeting and opposed something. He had also frequently telephoned Joe to gripe, and he had written letters to the local newspaper. Joe observed that at public meetings, the most maddening thing about Moe was that he always started out by saying, "My family has been in business in Warner Pier since my great-great-grandfather came here in 1845."

Joe said he always had an awful time not breaking in to comment, "So has my family, Moe, and none of us was ever very successful either."

Because despite the Davidson family's long history in southwest Michigan, no one in the clan ever became very prominent. They were farmers who didn't own much land, operators of barbershops and dry cleaning establishments, managers and clerks for small retail businesses. None of them was in "the professions"— law, medicine, theology, engineering, and such. Joe could never understand why Moe had thought an ordinary middle- and working-class background—even one covering one hundred seventy years—qualified him as an authority on civic affairs. A civics class would have been more impressive, and Moe hadn't even had that in his background.

Both Joe and I had also found Moe lacking in common sense. His positions on the city's doings seemed to come out of left field, or sometimes right field. One time he'd be strongly pro-environment. When the next issue came up, he'd take the position that government was putting environmental issues in front of individual rights. No one could ever predict if he was going to be pro or con on any particular issue until they saw his name on the list of donors.

But despite his fanatic and sometimes fantastic views on how to run the city, Moe had never run for office; he had lived outside the city limits. He'd simply remained an interested local businessman and public-spirited citizen who always got up and spoke his piece. By doing this, he'd managed to infuriate everybody at one time or another.

Moe might have been run out of town if it weren't for his clown act. Because when Moe shut up, he had truly been funny. At every community parade, carnival, or celebration, he had painted on a smile, put on his Hobo Moe costume, and made all the children—and most of the adults—laugh. As long as he kept his mouth shut, he had been hilarious.

Moe Davidson had been a strange combination of qualities, so maybe it was poetic justice that he had died strangely and that his death had led to a strange phone call.

I probably would have forgotten the whole thing—call, killing, and clown—if three things hadn't happened.

First, Aunt Nettie and Hogan took their dream trip to the South Sea Islands.

Second, a FOR SALE sign went up next door.

Third, Joe was dragged into the case.

Or maybe he jumped in willingly.

In midwinter in Michigan, we all dream of the South Seas.

This winter Aunt Nettie and Hogan had actually splurged on their dream trip—Samoa and Tahiti—and they were going in late February. No phones. Limited e-mail. Hogan found a retired sheriff's deputy to stand in as police chief, and Nettie and Hogan began to pack lightweight clothes in flowery patterns.

As usual, TenHuis Chocolade and I were both up to our ears in the annual winter promotion of the Chamber of Commerce tourism committee. This year the theme was Clown Week, so our shop was full of foil-wrapped molded clowns and molded clown hats in one-inch, two-inch, and four-inch sizes.

A few days after the strange phone call, Joe and I drove Hogan and Aunt Nettie to the Grand Rapids airport and enviously waved as they lugged their carry-ons down to the departure gate. When they reached Sydney they e-mailed to let us know they arrived safely and were about to set sail.

Their first day at sea was the day Moe Davidson's store went on the market.

As business manager of TenHuis Chocolade, I had long lusted after the building next door.

Moe Davidson had owned that building, but I didn't know who had inherited it. He was survived by a wife, Emma, and he had two grown children from a previous marriage. The Warner Pier gossip mill reported that Moe and the kids had hardly spoken for years. Both son and daughter were in their early thirties. I hadn't ever seen Moe's daughter, but I had heard that her name was Lorraine. I had met the son, Chuck, briefly, when he visited the shop.

Emma and Moe had been married about two years, and she had occasionally worked in the Clowning Around shop, but nobody in Warner Pier knew her well. The Davidsons hadn't spent the past two winters in Warner Pier; lots of tourist-oriented businesses close up in the off-season. Emma and Moe had gone to her home in Indiana. In addition, Emma hadn't taken much part in local affairs when she was there. I'd never met her, and I'd heard she didn't have much to say for herself.

Even though I didn't know just who now owned the building next door, I knew I wanted to buy it from them. So the new FOR SALE sign got my attention.

I thought TenHuis had lots of potential for expansion, and to expand we needed more space. I needed a larger office staff, but we had no place to put desks or people. We needed at least one sales rep out there calling on corporations and convention planners. We needed a larger shipping department. We needed a catalog and direct-mail department, a catering specialist, a larger work-room for producing truffles and bonbons, and a dozen other things that we couldn't have because we had no place to house them.

So I'd had my eye on the store next door as an investment for TenHuis Chocolade ever since I came to work for Aunt Nettie. It would double our available space while keeping TenHuis in its prime location, in the heart of Warner Pier's picturesque business district. However, I had always thought of the building as a purchase for TenHuis as a company. But the company couldn't buy a piece of property without Aunt Nettie's approval. She is president of the company.

But if the building went on sale while Aunt Nettie was out of the country, and I had to move quickly to get it—well, I might have to buy it on my own.

The thought was terrifying. I'd have to talk to Joe, of course, since he'd be linked to me as a purchaser. But it was probably doable. I fought down a panic attack, took two deep breaths, and called the Realtor.

That the sign even went up showed how out of touch Moe Davidson's kids—or wife, or whoever was handling his estate—were. Warner Pier is small enough to rely on word of mouth. If a piece of property in the business district goes on the market, the rest of the business community gets advance warning in the post office line or the drugstore or the coffee shop. Rarely do we find out something's for sale by seeing a sign.

At least the name of the real estate firm was familiar. I'd served on a Chamber of Commerce committee with the local agent, Tilda VanAust.

I saw the sign at ten thirty, and was on the phone with Tilda by ten thirty-five.

"How did the Davidsons get the store on the market so fast?" I asked.

"Actually," Tilda said, "Moe had signed the property over to Emma for tax reasons, so it didn't have to go through probate. Emma's signing it back to Chuck and Lorraine. She's here to help them close the building out, but she won't share in the proceeds."

"Interesting. How much are they asking?"

I held my breath. The asking price she mentioned was, of course, way too high, but I told her I'd definitely like to view the property.

I tried to sound cool. "Of course, Tilda, you know that business was not so hot this year in Warner Pier. But my aunt and I would like to consider expansion at some future date. So we might look at it as an investment."

"Lee, you know that this property is in a prime location. There's been a lot of interest in it already. I'm expecting an offer this week."

Sure. As if I believed that, since nobody had known it was going on the market. But now that it was officially for sale, I expected Tilda would be getting some calls. I definitely wanted to be first in line, but I didn't want to act so eager Tilda saw me as a sucker.

Tilda said she had some time that very day, so we agreed to tour the building at three o'clock.

As soon as I hung up I tried to figure out what time it was for Aunt Nettie and Hogan. Actually, I decided, it didn't matter. The best way to reach them was by e-mail. Hogan had said he'd check that whenever he had access to it. I fired off an electronic message.

Then I sat back and faced facts. I was on my own. It was unlikely that I'd be able to reach Aunt Nettie to get her approval in the next few days.

If I wanted advice, I had a perfectly good husband, who had a law degree and also knew a lot about construction. Joe would be glad to advise me. Besides, if I had to act on my own, any buying I did would involve him legally, so he'd have to go along with it anyway.

Joe works three days a week for an agency similar to the Legal Aid Society. It's located in Holland, thirty miles away, and specializes in poverty law. I picked up the phone and called his office.

"Sorry, Lee," the administrative assistant said. "He had to go see a judge down in Warner County. You could call his cell."

"I don't want to do that. Either he'd have it turned off or I'd interrupt something he doesn't want interrupted. I'll send him a text. But if you hear from him, ask him to call me."

I hung up and began to chew my nails and consider the possibilities.

I might not be able to talk the Davidson family down to a figure I thought was fair, and I'd have to give the whole project up. But even if we did reach an agreement, Aunt Nettie might not think it was a good idea.

Or if I couldn't reach Aunt Nettie, I could decide to buy it on my own, only to find that Aunt Nettie didn't want it.

Joe and I would wind up owning a downtown building we didn't really want. Then we could either resell it or rent it out. It might be a good financial investment.

Or we could fail to find a buyer or a leaser and lose a lot of money we couldn't afford to lose.

Looking at the purchase from several angles, I realized it could be either a real winner or a serious loser. I bit another nail.

When the time came to meet Tilda, I asked one of the ladies who make the chocolate to watch the counter. I also told her where I'd be and asked her to pass that news on to Joe if he showed up. Then I took a deep breath, put on my jacket, and headed next door.

The entrance to Clowning Around was ajar, so I walked right in, then came to a complete stop.

All I could see were clowns. Clown dolls, clown masks, clown puppets, clown pictures, clown books. They hung from the ceiling and were stacked in shelves along both side walls. They were piled on tables in the middle of the room. There were white-faced clowns, hobo clowns, even a mannequin of a dog wearing a clown costume. There were girl clowns and boy clowns. Harlequins and Pierrots. And the centerpiece was a large portrait of Moe himself, wearing his "Hobo Moe" outfit.

Crazy colors and wild shapes were everywhere. The bizarre decor of the shop made the first sound I heard fit right in. It was a loud, piercing whine. The noise sounded like a siren, but I quickly realized it was a human voice of the high-pitched and annoying sort.

"Honestly! The mess! This place is nowhere near ready to show to potential buyers. That agent must be crazy."

A deep and melodious male voice replied, "Cleaning is our responsibility, Lorraine. It's not up to the Realtor. And I'm not getting rid of anything until we get through this Clown Week promotion and see if we can't sell most of the stock."

"Nobody would buy those idiotic clowns! God! I've gotten to the point I hate these things. They're just reminders of what a jerk we had for a dad. And nobody will be interested in the building in the shape it's in. It needs to be staged."

"Staged?" The deep voice chuckled. "You've been watching too much HGTV."

"You haven't been watching enough, Chuck. Things have to look attractive if they're going to sell."

I'd apparently interrupted a family quarrel. I quickly slammed the door behind me, just to make a noise, then called out, "Hello! Anybody here?"

I heard a gasp from the back room, and the face of a blond woman appeared between two clown masks. The light was so lousy I couldn't see her clearly, but when she spoke the voice was the one I'd heard earlier.

"Hi, there! Are you Mrs. Woodyard?"

"Yes, I'm Lee Woodyard, your next-door neighbor. I was supposed to meet Tilda VanAust."

"She got held up, so she sent us to open up. I'm Lorraine Davidson."

The woman edged out of a curtained door, which obviously led to the back room. She hit a switch and light flooded over her. The effect was that one of the clowns had come to life.

Lorraine was one of these women who apparently believe that if a little makeup enhances her appearance, then a lot will make her a raving beauty. She wore heavy blue eye shadow, and blush was slathered on in exactly the wrong part of her cheeks. Her eyebrows looked as if they'd been painted on with a Magic Marker. Her hair had been bleached until it would have tempted any healthy horse to have a bite, and she wore it in a fluffy "big hair" style.

In other words, her appearance matched her voice. Loud, brassy, and unpleasant.

I blinked. Then I saw a man behind her and realized it must be the guy with the voice as melodious as Lorraine's was raucous.

"Hi," he said. "I'm Chuck Davidson."

Chuck matched his voice, too. He was tall, nice-looking, and neatly dressed, with dark hair and even features. He came forward and we shook hands. He had a pleasant smile.

"And this," Chuck said, "is our stepmother, Emma."

For a moment I couldn't figure out who he was talking about. There was no other person present. Then there was movement among the clowns, and a small woman came from behind the counter.

Mrs. Davidson couldn't have offered a greater contrast to her stepdaughter. Lorraine was tall. Emma Davidson was short. Lorraine was thin, almost skinny. Mrs. Davidson was plump. Lorraine had long bleached hair. Her stepmom's hair was a mousy brown and was short and straight.

Mrs. Davidson didn't speak, but simply nodded.

I hadn't come to talk to these people. I hoped I'd greeted them pleasantly, but I was there to look around.

So we looked. I told the three of them that I wanted to get an idea of the building and to visualize the changes that would be required if we expanded into that space. I led the way, looking at the shelving, then going into the back to judge the amount of room. I had brought a flashlight, and I investigated the basement, making sure there were no damp spots and taking a look at the furnace. Chuck accompanied me. I addressed questions to him, but he was vague about details such as utility bills and taxes. I'd have to get those figures from Tilda.

I wasn't paying him much mind, actually, until he caught my attention with a strange remark.

"Of course, I know that cost is no object to you, Lee."

I turned to look at him, and I'm sure my amazement showed. But I tried to turn my reply into a joke. "Chuck! I'm an accountant! I assure you that if my last name was Rockefeller, cost would matter to me."

He smiled. "I know you and your husband are major benefactors of Warner Pier."

For a moment I felt more amazed than ever. Then I got it. "Oh. Someone has told you that Joe donated the Warner Point Conference Center to the city."

"It was a terrific gift."

"Joe inherited that property unexpectedly, and he didn't want to own it. In fact, because of the taxes and upkeep he couldn't afford to own it. He says he gained financially by giving it away. And he donated it with the understanding that his name would never appear publicly in connection with the center."

"I'm sorry! I didn't know the background."

"That's quite all right. There's no secret about any of this. But I assure you that Joe and I personally are like most people. We live paycheck to paycheck. As for the possible purchase of this building, that would be a business decision for TenHuis Chocolade. I certainly have no interest in becoming a downtown landowner myself."

I had to admire Chuck. Although I had tried to speak pleasantly, I had definitely told him where to get off. A lot of people would have been crushed by my little speech. Chuck didn't turn a hair.

"I'm sorry I misunderstood the situation. I guess I'm used to my dad."

"Your dad?"

"Oh, yes. I'm sure you know he was always giving

money for community projects. But he would want full credit and a picture in the newspaper."

I'd observed that particular trait in Moe myself. But I decided I'd better not comment.

"I guess I'm ready to look around upstairs," I said. "Is the stairway near the rear entrance?"

Chuck followed me to the back. I had stopped for a look at the staff bathroom when I heard the front door open. Good, I thought, it's Tilda. Now we can get down to cases.

Instead, I heard Lorraine's raucous croak. "Of all the nerve!"

The voice that replied to her was deep and familiar. "I beg your pardon?"

"You've got gall, coming here to harass us!"

"I'm sorry—I was told I would find my wife here."

It was Joe, and for some reason Lorraine Davidson was very angry with him.

JoAnna Carl
The Chocoholic Mystery Series

EACH BOOK INCLUDES YUMMY CHOCOLATE TRIVIA!

Looking for a fresh start, divorcée Lee McKinney moves back to Michigan to work for her aunt's chocolate business—and finds that her new job offers plenty of murderous treats.

Available wherever books are sold or at
penguin.com

facebook.com/TheCrimeSceneBooks

OM0031